Defiance

A Historical Romance

Defiance

A Historical Romance

G.G. Vandagriff

Other Books by G.G. Vandagriff

Historical Fiction

The Last Waltz—New Edition

Exile

Regency Romance

Lord John's Dilemma

Lord Grenville's Choice

The Baron and The Bluestocking

Lord Trowbridge's Angel

Rescuing Rosalind

Miss Braithwaite's Secret

The Taming of Lady Kate

The Duke's Undoing

Women's Fiction

The Only Way to Paradise

Pieces of Paris

Suspense

The Arthurian Omen—New Edition

Foggy with a Chance of Murder

Alex and Briggie Mysteries

The Hidden Branch – New Edition

Tangled Roots—New Edition

Poisoned Pedigree—New Edition

Of Deadly Descent—New Edition

Cankered Roots—New Edition

Non-Fiction

Deliverance from Depression

Voices In Your Blood: Discovering Identity Through Family History

{ 1 }

May 1940
Oxford, England

Rudi von Schoenenburg walked into the crowded pub, stopping to inhale its comforting smell of beer and chips. He *needed* to see Hannah. Sometimes she still came here, and he hoped today would be one of those days. The Eagle and Child had figured largely in their late romance. As he looked over the pub's patrons, he searched for her shiny brunette head among the inglenooks.

There. Could that be Hannah? Moving through the crowds toward the back of the pub, he found the woman he sought sitting alone on a bench against the wall, staring into her pint. Her hair fell in waves over one side of her face, lending her an unconscious glamour. For a moment, he just stood and looked at her as his heart swelled with too much emotion. He was iron to her magnet. It seemed he had loved her forever, but it was only just two years, and most of that time they had spent apart at her request. But occasionally there were days like today where she showed up out of the blue, knowing right where to find him at this hour.

He seated himself next to her. "Hello, Hannah."

"Rudi!" Looking up with a beaming smile, she threw an arm around his neck and kissed his cheek. "I knew you would come."

Surprised by her demonstrativeness, he pulled away slightly and looked into her face. Her brows quickly drew together in a frown and tears sprang to her eyes. He had never known her to cry.

"What is it?"

"It's Papa. He died this morning."

He wrapped his arm around her shoulders and pulled her against his side. "This is sudden, isn't it?" He could feel her sadness spilling into him, tugging down his spirits. Hannah and her father had enjoyed a relationship he had often envied. But it surprised him that she had sought him out in such a circumstance.

"Cancer of the pancreas. He kept quiet about the pain. We only found out two weeks ago, and now, suddenly, he's gone."

Unable to help himself, he brought his unoccupied hand up to her smooth, pale cheek and used his thumb to wipe away a tear that had fallen. "I'm so sorry, *Liebchen*." Her espresso-colored eyes were even more beautiful with her tears starring her lashes.

She looked back into her drink, now avoiding his eyes. "I'm sure you can understand. You lost your father even more suddenly. I'm full of so many emotions I can't describe."

Rudi's mind immediately flashed back to the murderous scene played out in a snowstorm in the Austrian Alps. Two years ago, during his family's escape from Austria, he had watched his father being gunned down by four members of Hitler's SS.

"There's grief and anger and melancholy," he said. "But there's also the whole sense that it didn't really happen. That the world couldn't possibly have changed that much."

"Yes. You're exactly right. In addition to losing Papa, I am beginning to feel that my whole world is falling apart." She swirled the beer in her glass, looking into its depths. "Before today, everything in my life was set. My trajectory was clear. But now, it all stretches out for miles and miles like an open sea. I have no compass."

Was it possible that she was questioning her engagement? Rudi felt a spurt of hope, but tamped it down. "I know your father had great hopes for you."

Looking up at him, her eyes were pleading. "Oh, Rudi . . . how can Samuel and I ever be a family without Papa? We all got along so well. But with Mama already dead, now there will just be Samuel and me. And . . ." She averted her eyes, leaving her sentence hanging.

Rudi's heart had been in hibernation ever since that day two years before when she had told him that for her father's sake, she could only marry a Jew. Now all it took was a small hope to revive it again. "For most couples love between the two of them is enough," he observed quietly.

She turned her glass in her hands. "He is a very worthy man, Rudi. A good Jew, a brilliant philosopher with a good career as a professor, and he loves me. My father expected me to marry a Jew."

"I know all that, Hannah."

"I am supposed to be married next month. He was like a son to Papa."

Rudi held up her chin with his fingers so she was forced to look at him, eyes full of pain. Her words came out in a whisper, as she wiped another tear. "With Papa dying, it's terrible. Do you understand?"

Everything in Rudi craved taking her face in his hands and kissing her with the pent up hunger of two years, but he knew his timing was wrong. Just because she didn't want to marry Samuel next month didn't really mean anything. Overwhelming grief would put anyone off. But at least she had come to him for comfort. He pulled her against his chest once more, speaking low into her hair. "Of course I understand, sweetheart. It makes perfect sense. I believe I can even sense the depths of your grief. I am told fathers and daughters have a special bond. You really must feel cast adrift."

"We were only renting the cottage. I no longer have a home."

"What about the penicillin study? Are you still working on that?"

Hannah tossed her hair out of her face. "There is a group of top-notch scientists working on it now. They've made great progress. Things are looking tremendously hopeful. But they don't really need me anymore. I'm rather underfoot." She ran the fingers of one hand over the rolled collar of his sweater. "Biochemistry is my profession, but I realize my identity has always been very tied up with my family and our traditions. Now I am alone."

In all the time since he had met her on the docks at Lake Zurich, Rudi never recalled having seen Hannah at a loss. She had always been assertive and forward-looking, even when her lab had been tossed by a Nazi lunatic who had tried to kill them both. Though he wanted to comfort her, he mostly felt a desire to recall her to her own strength.

She nibbled her bottom lip. "I prayed you were not already fighting in France. I have been sitting here weeping into my beer."

Was she really so attached to him? The idea came as a not unwelcome surprise. He wished for a moment that he had better news for her. He took her chin in his hands. "*Liebchen,* on the first of June, I report as a fighter pilot in the RAF. I've already done my training. I came here today, hoping to see you one last time before I left."

She closed her eyes, taking a deep breath. When she had composed herself, she put her hand up to his cheek and stroked it. "I might have guessed. Only the most dangerous job for you."

"I feel it is what I am meant to be doing, Hannah."

"And you will be brilliant at it," she said, smiling at him tremulously.

"I will finally get a chance to shoot at some Germans. It has been a long time coming." He clenched his jaw.

"You will avenge your father's murder many times over, I am certain of it."

For a moment, they said nothing, then Rudi covered the hand still on his cheek. Its warmth was something he would be able to carry into battle—a precious gift. "I am sorry that I never got to meet your father. Will there be a memorial service?"

"It will be small. He didn't know many people in this country." Dropping her hand, she looked away.

He wanted to kiss her so much, it was painful. "Hannah." He brought her chin around so he could see her face again. "When it is over, come to London. I am leaving here in the morning for my mother's town home. Spend some time with me and my family before I report for duty. It will be good for you; it's not a time for you to be alone. And my family thinks the world of you. You know that."

Tears flooded her eyes again. "I would like that. I haven't seen your mother's new home."

He pulled a small notebook out of his pocket and, writing down the address, tore the page out and passed it to her. "She lives in Mayfair. There is a guest room that will suit you perfectly."

Looking at the small sheet of paper, she gave a little smile. "I'll do it, Rudi. I'll come, whatever Samuel has to say about it. I have never even met his family. They live in Birmingham."

At her words, his heart lifted. Perhaps there was a chance for them after all. "Stay where you are," he said. "I'll bring you another pint."

London
May 26, 1940

Though it was late afternoon on Sunday, Anthony Fotheringill had been called into work at the Foreign Office. Up to this point, they had heard very little about how the war was proceeding in France. It was past time for a bulletin. And from the sounds of it, it was not going to be a cheery one. The infernal German army had proved invincible ever since the invasion of Poland last September. Its spring offensive had been lethal, taking Norway, Denmark, and the Low Countries in almost a single gulp.

"Fotheringill?"

Anthony stopped in the hallway outside his office. Turning, he faced Nigel Reston, a fellow undersecretary and close personal friend. "Yes?"

"Halifax has called the meeting for half an hour from now."

"Right. Thanks. It should be interesting, at least."

His friend frowned. "Maybe we'll finally get some news. Word from the front has certainly been sparse."

"You're right. It's worrisome," Anthony replied. Reston was not one to let things get him down. But they both knew instinctively that the situation on the Continent was bad. The man walked away, hands in his pockets, looking down at the floor. "Blighted Nazis," he said.

Entering his office, Anthony settled behind his massive mahogany desk, picked up the telephone and rang The Laurels to let his friend Zaleski know that he might be late showing up at the house for a drink that evening.

Half an hour later, Anthony sat next to Reston in the conference room, waiting for the Foreign Secretary. They filled their pipes. Lord Halifax entered five minutes early, his high brow contracted, his eyes solemn. He eased his long frame into his chair and, clasping his hands on the table in front of him, he rotated his thumbs around one another, his withered hand in its usual black glove. Growing anxious at these signs, Anthony forked his fingers through his fair hair, willing the other undersecretaries to arrive.

When all were gathered, the Foreign Secretary cleared his throat and began. "I have very grave news from Mr. Eden and Mr. Churchill. The French and Belgians are not able to stabilize the Front. The British Expeditionary Force is pulling back to Dunkirk for the purpose of an evacuation. Needless to say, the War Cabinet is in an uproar."

The room's stunned silence echoed in Anthony's head. "They've only been fighting a few days! How could things have gotten so bad so quickly?"

"The Germans didn't attack at the Maginot Line as expected. They came through the Ardennes Forest. I know very few details. There has been little communication. Prime Minister Reynaud is very gloomy about the situation. And Mr. Eden told me this morning that the time has come when we must consider the grave position of our own forces. He agrees with our commander-in-chief, Lord Gort, and has told him that we must seriously think about evacuation. It is obvious that our troops must live to fight in our own defense."

Reston spoke. "This is grave news, indeed. Have we a hope of getting the troops home?"

"A one in a thousand chance, I should think," said the Foreign Secretary. "Everything is happening so fast, and as I said, the communication is very poor. Coordinating any kind of evacuation is going to be exceedingly difficult. Vice Admiral Ramsay has been put in charge. He's setting up housekeeping in the old corridors and rooms carved out of the chalk in Dover cliffs during Napoleon's time."

Anthony felt ill. How were they to fight on alone if their army was defeated, killed, or imprisoned in France? It seemed that an evacuation, no matter how difficult, was their only hope.

Halifax continued, "We must be very careful not to alarm the people, but the troops are being pushed back to Dunkirk and bombed by the Stukas. Their situation is grim, indeed. We have diverted as many ships as we can to Dunkirk, but even they have no idea what their orders are."

"I know Dunkirk, and it's not a proper port," said Wainright. "It's not any kind of place to evacuate an army. How are the troops to get from the beach to the ships?"

"That is one of many problems the Royal Navy is trying to solve. But we must take our cue from the Prime Minister and be optimistic that it *will* be solved. He has tremendous confidence in our navy.

"I have warned you of these eventualities because we will be in a unique position when France falls, as it looks like it must. If we succeed in evacuating our troops, the French will undoubtedly feel they were left in the lurch." He drummed the fingers of his right hand on the table. "Also, the Poles will most likely move their government here, and they are experiencing very turbulent relations with the Soviet Union at the moment. Our relations with Stalin are dicey as well. We will have our work cut out for us in the diplomacy arena. The Poles and Free French will still be our allies. Poland has evacuated a large portion of their remaining army. We want both France and Poland to aid us in our fight to defend this Island."

"Is the French army considering evacuation, as well?" asked Wainright.

"I imagine that if defeat should become even more inevitable, they will try something to preserve as much of their fighting force as possible. Pray that it will be so."

"We are bracing for an invasion," Colgrave said. It was not a question.

"We are," said Halifax. "But the government is taking one thing at a time. And now our priority is evacuation. But this news is not to go any further than this office. There are too many Nazi sympathizers out there, and of course we do not want to alarm the populace. I will be in touch with the French gov-

ernment and Sikorski, the Prime Minister of the Polish government-in-exile. I expect we will see them set up here within the
month."

Anthony left the Foreign Office that evening with a heavy
heart. At least Halifax was finally on board and not talking
about making a separate peace with Hitler. They needed unity
in the government to take on this Herculean task.

He gave himself a mental shake. If any country in the world
could defeat Hitler, it was Britain. But could they do it alone?

Having called ahead, he arrived at the Zaleski townhouse.
Simms, the butler, told him that he would find his friend in the
drawing room with madam and one other guest. Anthony
frowned. He hoped it was not to become a cocktail party. He
wasn't in the mood, nor was he properly dressed.

He need not have worried. Amalia—Zaleski's wife of eighteen
months whom Anthony still thought of as the Baroness von
Schoenenburg—was not in an evening gown, but a simple ivory
silk frock. As she walked across the white and gold room to
greet him, slender and deceptively fragile-looking, he thought
as he always did what a beautiful setting she had created for
herself in this lovely home. She had been through so much, not
the least of which was a harrowing escape from Austria and the
murder of her husband by the SS. But she had resurfaced and
made the very best of things. Seeing her under present circumstances gave him a lift. She offered her cheek for a kiss.

"Dear Anthony. I'm so happy you were able to get away after
all. We have a Polish guest staying with us that I'd like you to
meet. She has always been like a little sister to Andrzej. Their
families lived next door to one another," she said in her scarcely

accented English, putting her hand through his arm. "Would you care for whiskey—or perhaps a martini?" she asked.

"Whiskey, please. With a splash."

Amalia fixed his drink, and then guided him over to her husband, who was speaking to the young woman. "Nika is newly arrived from France. She left because she doesn't like the situation there."

In her graceful manner, Amalia introduced him to the very lovely brunette with a face that belonged on a cameo. It wore a haunted look. He only caught her first name: Dominika. Her last name was a slur of consonants. "Mr. Fotheringill speaks excellent French," Amalia told her.

Her husband indicated that he needed to speak to her, so she left the two of them together. Anthony was unaware of her going; he saw only the woman before him who was not as young as he first thought. She reminded him of gardenias with her smooth, white skin, and the light floral fragrance she wore.

He smiled at her and, knowing his social awkwardness in the presence of beautiful women was probably showing, offered her his hand.

"My surname was not meant for the English tongue," she said to him in beautiful French. "Please call me Nika."

"I am Anthony," he replied. "It is a pleasure to meet you." Casting about for something clever to say, he added. "I understand you have just arrived from France."

"Yes. The war is not going well there, Anthony. I fear the Germans are unstoppable." Her eyes filled with tears and she put a hand to her forehead. "It is the *Blitzkrieg* on Poland all over again."

After fortifying himself with a sip of his whiskey, he said, "But you are safe in England now."

Nika nodded and, pulling a handkerchief from her sleeve, she dabbed her eyes. "Yes. I am safe. For now."

How should he respond to these tears? He became gruff. "You must take heart, Nika and stop your tears. We are a nation of bulldogs. We do our best when we are up against it." Just saying the words made him feel better, himself. Clearing his throat while she gained control over her tears, he sought more solid ground. "So. You are staying here with the Zaleskis?"

"Yes, they have been very kind to take me in. Andrzej lived with his Uncle Paul in the home next to ours in Warsaw." She cast her eyes down. "My family is all dead now."

Anthony felt a stroke of compassion so strong, it made him ashamed of his discomfort and softened his heart. He lost his awkwardness. Though he longed to comfort the woman, he hadn't the words. He asked softly, "How did you escape?"

"I hardly know. The bombing of Warsaw was more relentless than you can imagine. The army and even the populace fought bravely. We made a barricade of streetcars and every other vehicle available. But food began to run out. And there were hardly any places left to take shelter. My parents and I had decided to try to reach Hungary. We had a guide who was going to take a number of us." Her voice trembled and she paused for a moment. When she resumed, her eyes were fixed on the carpet. "The night before we were to leave, the bombs hit our house. We were in the basement, but a beam crashed across my parents, killing them instantly. My brother had already been killed at the beginning of the fighting. I left the next day with the clothes on my back." She blew her nose. "Somehow our group made it to Hungary." Wiping another tear away, she said, "I had friends in Paris at the *Sorbonne*. They sent me money for the journey to France. I was there teaching at the *Sorbonne* myself until yesterday."

He turned the glass in his hands, searching for words. "I am truly sorry. I cannot imagine what it would be like to lose your home and family and country all at once," he said, his voice gentle. When she said nothing, he studied her downturned face. It was heart-shaped with high Slavic cheekbones, a narrow nose, and full lips. He judged her to be in her late thirties. Fighting against his basic instinct to rescue her, he told himself that any relationship with this woman could not possibly end well. She was probably too young for his forty-five years, even if he hadn't been divorced. The Poles were Roman Catholics. Roman Catholics frowned on divorce. These things raced through his mind— excuses for his real problem. He was powerfully attracted to the woman, to both her bravery and her vulnerability.

"I lost no more than every other Pole that I know," she was saying, her voice now firm. "Do you know why the Warsawians fought so hard?"

Anthony feared he knew the answer, but he shook his head.

"We were told that the British and the French had engaged the Germans on the Western Front. That the war would be a short one and the Germans would be compelled to surrender any day."

Guilt swamped him. "The Royal Navy did take action," he said. "But I agree that that was hardly enough. Poland made an incredible showing. I wish that this country had been in position to attack Germany from the west. But, we were unprepared. Had Mr. Churchill been in office then as he is now, the war would have been stopped before it began—in Czechoslovakia."

G.G. Vandagriff

Looking up into his eyes at last, she said, "I don't know why I've felt it necessary to confide all this. I don't usually talk about it. No one wants to hear our sad tale."

Her tearfulness wrung his heart. He shuffled his stance. "I'm glad you did, Nika. It occurs to me that perhaps I can help you to get a teaching position."

"However could you do that?" she asked, wiping her eyes again.

"My sister teaches at Somerville, a women's college in Oxford. What subject did you teach at the *Sorbonne?*"

"I have a doctorate in Slavic literature and languages."

He gave her what he hoped was an encouraging smile. "I doubt there are too many of those floating about. Irene teaches the Greek and Roman Classics. I am certain she would like to meet you, at the very least. She is very fond of Tolstoy."

Amalia and Andrzej rejoined them in time to hear his offer. "Anthony is also like family," their hostess told Nika. "He and Andrzej fought together in the Great War and he took us in when we came to this country. He can be a great help to you."

Halifax's news about the evacuation of the British Expeditionary Force had been jolted from his mind by the beautiful Polish woman, but now, seeing Zaleski and remembering all they had been through together, the war news returned to his mind. He implored Nika, "Tell us about what is happening in France."

She moistened her lips. "Well, the Parisians can't seem to take it in. Most of them still have faith in the army, still believe it is the strongest in Europe. They wait daily for the news that they have thrown back the Germans. But there is a growing minority that is very alarmed. I am sure you realize that the

French have put all their faith in the Maginot Line of fortresses, which Hitler avoided altogether."

"Yes," Zaleski said, joining in the conversation. "That was unexpected. But one can count on Hitler for that." Anthony's friend was his usual self, darkly handsome with the looks of a matinee idol. He found himself wondering if Nika had once had a schoolgirl crush on him.

"I would say that they should have been prepared," Nika said. "Like the French, we Poles pride ourselves on our great, brave hearts, but when all was and done, that was not enough. Some cities fought to virtual extinction, to no purpose." Nika's face was pale with sadness.

Anthony said, "The *Blitzkrieg* offense is unprecedented in warfare, Nika. The world has never seen anything like it." He drew himself up and said heartily, "We are now manufacturing tanks and fighter planes as quickly as we can turn them out."

Zaleski frowned and said, "They are needed in France, and soon. I don't think we really have the full picture of what is going on there. It is happening so fast. It is as unlike the Great War as it can be."

"Poland fell in a month," Nika said, her face tragic.

Remembering Halifax's news, Anthony wondered if France would even hold on that long.

{ 2 }

Hannah threw a fistful of dirt down upon her father's casket, tears streaking her face. Moments later, she left the small Jewish cemetery on Samuel's arm, resigned to the unsubstantial feel of his support. Her fiancé was only her height, and slight of build. So different from Rudi's muscular frame. But this was no time to be thinking those thoughts. She climbed into the limousine provided by the funeral home and was silent during their drive back to Oxford. Samuel kept up a monologue upon some obscure philosophical point concerning Judaism and the state of the universe. She knew it was meant to be comforting, but she tuned him out, wondering how soon she could leave for London. Dabbing at her face with her handkerchief, she told herself she needed a complete change of scene.

She felt unusually vulnerable. It wasn't just losing Papa, it was the war. Soon Rudi would be in the skies in a fragile aircraft, swooping high above the Channel, shooting and getting shot at.

I will feel better if I have something to do. Perhaps I shall join the WAAFS.

Breaking in on Samuel's elegant theorem, she said, "I am going to London. I am going to join the WAAFs."

"What are the WAAFs?" he asked, his nearly black eyes curious and steady as they regarded her. Samuel was undeniably handsome with his wavy black hair, chiseled chin, and beautiful lips. He was also endlessly patient and kind.

"The Women's Auxiliary Air Force," she replied.

His brow furrowed as he asked, "And our wedding, dearest?"

"Perhaps they will give me leave," she said. "I must do something, Samuel, or I will lose my mind."

"I understand that, Hannah, but must it be something military in nature?"

All her tears had left her raw, without the strength to be diplomatic. She removed her hand from his arm. "To be frank, yes. I don't share your pacifist politics. You know that."

"I understand, and frankly, it troubles me more than a bit." He continued frowning.

How could he be such an ostrich? "You have always lived in England. You do not really understand what a threat the Nazis are to the Jews. They *killed* our neighbor and rabbi in Zurich. They *killed* my brother, Samuel."

"I always thought they killed him because he was a socialist."

"A member of the Nazi party killed him, for whatever reason. There was a witness. We didn't flee Austria because we are socialists. We fled because we are Jews. We fled Switzerland for the same reason. You know Hitler is a raving anti-Semite. If he invades this country, your little bubble will burst, Samuel."

He raised an eyebrow. "What little bubble?"

"The one you live in. The bubble of denial."

They had arrived at the cottage, hers for only a few more days. Samuel helped her out of the car. As she rooted through her handbag for her keys, he said, "I believe you're being deliberately provoking."

Opening her door, she entered and immediately smelled Papa's pipe tobacco. Tears started again, and she whirled on her fiancé. "There is a whole world out there, Samuel. It's messy. It can't be defined by theorems. Tradition won't hold it in bounds!"

Startled, he could only stare at her.

"It is my nature to be in the thick of things, not standing on the sidelines," she said.

His voice was unexpectedly tender as he said, "It's one of the things I love about you, Hannah. I also admire your straightforwardness. I don't want you to change in any way."

"Even if what I know to be true is directly counter to your beliefs?"

Pulling her close, he kissed her on the forehead. "We will postpone the wedding if needs must. You go to London and get this out of your system."

He made her sound like a willful child. Hannah stifled a sarcastic reply. "I must go pack."

Amalia awoke early, her body curled into Andrzej's. For a moment she drew in the sensation of him pressed against every inch of her. Even after a year and a half, she still did not take his presence for granted. Her heart still swelled each morning when she woke like this, filled with tenderness and the depth of a love created from years of being buried in the well of her consciousness. With her marriage, parts of her had been reborn, flowering in new colors and sensations. She had never been so happy.

Then, blasting through her contentment, came new worries: Christian, days away from the end of his term at Oxford, intending to join MI5. Rudi about to join the RAF with its enormous casualty rate.

Moving carefully so as not to wake Andrzej, she rose and pulled on her dressing gown. She went next door to her sitting room and rang for her morning chocolate. From her window, she looked out upon another gray May day. Still, after two years, she missed Vienna and the home she had left. But the Nazis had come, killed Rudolf, and chased her from everything that was familiar. Now that her English had improved and she didn't feel so isolated, London was growing on her, but it would never be Vienna. That golden age—when she and Andrzej had met and fallen in love before the Great War—was gone forever.

Her husband had lost his homeland as well. It had been seven months since Poland had fallen at the hands of double foes— Germany and the Soviet Union, who had partitioned it between them. She and Andrzej had both vowed to do whatever they could to stop Hitler. Her sons, of enlistment age, were full of "vim and vinegar," as the British might say, anxious to take up the fight. But Amalia knew that war was not glorious. After nursing soldiers through the last war, she knew war to be lethal, muddy, and bloody.

Though no one wanted to stop Hitler more than she, Amalia almost wished that Churchill had not seen to a special dispensation for her boys, Austrian citizens, to join the RAF and MI5 at the Home Office. But they would have been miserable watching from the sidelines. Ever since the midnight bloodbath in the snowy Alps, they had been looking forward to the time when they could avenge their father's death. They had grown up in the shadow of Hitler's Germany, the violence of the Austrian Nazis, and their father's never ending efforts as a cabinet minister to steer their government in a democratic direction. Though they had accepted Andrzej as a friend, no one would ever replace their father as mentor and hero.

Amalia's chocolate came and, while sipping it she perused her closet for something professional looking. She decided on a sage green suit with a cream silk blouse and a pillbox hat. Today, she and Andrzej were headed to Southwark across the Thames to offer their services as a nurse and surgeon to Guy's Hospital for the duration of the war. They both felt that an air war over the Channel was inevitable. Even now, there were some injured pilots who had managed to nurse their planes back across the Channel being treated there.

Andrzej joined her, holding a mug of coffee. He parted the hair on the back of her neck and kissed her gently. Setting her chocolate down, she offered him her lips, and they kissed warmly. "Did you remember that Rudi said Hannah is to come down from Oxford today?" he asked.

"I thought we were going to Guy's," she said.

"Her train doesn't arrive until this afternoon. We will have time this morning."

"I am anxious to see her again, but last I heard, she was engaged."

Andrzej drew his fingers through her mass of wavy mahogany hair. He had always adored it, ever since they had first fallen in love when she was nineteen. She put her head against his chest, relishing the sensation.

He continued, "Rudi doesn't know anything about that situation, he says, but he convinced her to come to London for a while. Her father just died and she is at loose ends."

"It is telling that she wanted to come to us at such a time, don't you think?"

"Perhaps," he said. "I don't know anything about her fiancé. Maybe she needs to feel part of a family at this time."

Guy's was one of the oldest hospitals in London, and the primary teaching hospital. Amalia was enchanted with its beautiful Palladian architecture and courtyards. They had an appointment with an assistant administrator, Mr. Harold Bussman, who took them on a tour of the up-to-date facilities and modern operating theaters. After hearing of their years of work at the University Hospital in Vienna, he agreed with Andrzej's assessment of the future demands this hospital could face.

"No one appears to be able to stop Hitler. He's not going to give up any time soon. We already have half a ward full of flyers."

Amalia's stomach clenched. Would she be treating her own son here one day? Would he lie in this hospital with bandaged eyes and limbs—her big, active auburn-haired Rudi? Pushing the thought away with difficulty, she listened as Andrzej told Mr. Bussman of their medical experiences in the last war.

Mr. Bussman replied, "It will be good to have professionals of your experience working here."

After the tour, they filled out detailed applications and were told that one of the doctors would call them to set up interviews. Traveling home to Mayfair by taxi, they were both silent in their reflections. Amalia shivered. She couldn't help but think of the last war.

"Andrzej, how did Anthony lose his leg? Were you fighting with him then?"

"Poor fellow. It was one of those random things. Could have happened to any of us. I was right near him when a grenade was lobbed into the trench landing right on top of his foot. It shattered everything up to his femur. Luckily, they were able to save his upper leg, but it was a close thing."

"How dreadful. The poor man. But he manages very well."

"It was harder on him emotionally than physically."

A vision suddenly assailed Amalia: Rudi flying his fragile Spitfire, shot up by gunfire, spiraling into the Channel. The war suddenly seemed very near.

Rudi's heart pinged off his ribs as Hannah descended from the Oxford train. Sighting him, she smiled broadly and waved. He went to her and, after a brotherly kiss on the cheek, took her suitcase.

"Mother and Andrzej are anxious to see you. I'm so glad you decided to come."

"It is such a relief to be away from Oxford and that cottage. It smells like Papa's pipe." She put her hand through his arm. "Oh, Rudi, it is so *good* to see you."

An inquisitive devil prompted him to ask, "How did you leave Samuel?"

"He was surprisingly understanding. I shouldn't say surprisingly, I suppose. He is amazingly tolerant of me."

"I hope he is something more than tolerant," Rudi said.

"Let's not talk of Samuel," Hannah said with a little toss of her head.

"That's fine with me. Have I told you I like your hair down like that? Very Veronica Lake."

"Now that I'm no longer working at the clinic, I'm going for glamour," she said.

"So you've finished up there?" Rudi took the taxi at the head of the queue, handing the suitcase to the driver.

"Yes. And I have a surprise for you. I'm joining the WAAFs!"

A spurt of joy jumped through Rudi. "As the Brits say, 'Jolly good,' Hannah!"

"I shall try to be posted by your airfield. Do you know where you will be yet?"

"Somewhere in the southeast. That's where I'd like to be."

"How like you. Then I shall try to be posted there. I have no idea if they'll take my wishes into account, but I will try."

Rudi was touched. Such concern for him was undoubtedly a good sign. But it still didn't make him Jewish. Clearing his throat, he changed the subject. "I should tell you we have another guest. Dominika something. She is from Poland by way of Hungary and France. She survived the *Blitzkrieg*. I was talking to her about it last night. It sounds like a dreadful bloodbath. It is incredible that the Poles were able to hold out for a month. Especially with the Soviets invading through the backdoor, just when things were at their worst."

"I assume she knows your stepfather?"

"Just call him Dr. Zaleski. I'm still not comfortable calling him my stepfather."

"I'm sorry, Rudi. Do you get along?" Her forehead furrowed with a concern that touched him.

"Splendidly. We are friends. He treats me as an equal. I am too old to be taking on another father figure."

"I am glad you are friends, at least. How is your mother?"

"Anxious about Chris and me, though she tries not to show it. She really is splendid, you know." He looked out the window, recognizing the white stone townhouse with the green shutters. "And here we are." It felt good to be bringing Hannah home.

His mother greeted her with genuine warmth. "Hannah, dear, we were so saddened to hear about your father. We are so glad you are to stay with us for a bit."

Hannah teared up at the gentle words. Rudi watched as she blinked rapidly and replied, "It is so lovely to be in your beautiful home. It reminds me of Vienna, with all the gold and white."

"You couldn't have said anything that would have pleased me more," his mother said.

After Hannah was settled in the guest room next to Nika's, the four of them sat to tea in the yellow sitting room. With the war rations, it was only bread and butter and apricot jam from Anthony's country estate, but the tradition was one his mother had embraced. The conversation contained a mixture of French and English.

Rudi announced, "Hannah is to join the WAAFs."

His mother said, "Splendid!" Then, she translated the conversation into French for Nika, presumably explaining the meaning of *WAAFs*.

A conversation ensued between Nika and Amalia in French, which Rudi could not understand. He turned to Hannah, "We will take you down to RAF headquarters tomorrow and get you signed up. I hate to see you so downcast. I know it's natural, but I'd like to help you through it, if I can."

"You help me through it just by being you. I love your family. In spite of everything you have been through, you are so positive."

Rudi chanced it and took her hand in his. "You have been through a great deal as well, and I have always thought of you the same way. The intensity of your grief will pass, Hannah. It will take time, but your war work will help. And, of course, my family and I will do all we can to support you."

She didn't pull her hand away. "I am so glad you didn't say 'cheer you up.' Losing Papa has been a blow in so many ways. I have no family left, Rudi."

"For as long as you want, you have the von Schoenenburgs."

She smiled through her tears.

The following day did not go according to plan. Mid-morning Andrzej received a telephone call from Tough Brothers, the boatyard on the Thames where *A New Day*, the Zaleski family yacht was docked. He was asked to come down to the Port Authority Tower on urgent business for the His Majesty's Government. Curious, Rudi and Hannah asked to join him.

"What in the world could the government want with a fifty-foot yacht?" Rudi asked.

"Curious, indeed," Andrzej agreed. "But it must have something to do with the war effort."

When they arrived, the docks were shrouded in heavy mist. They met with a milling group of boat owners coming in and out of the tower. Everyone seemed equally mystified. Finally reaching a man in the uniform of the Royal Navy, they were told to "grab their gear and food for a few days." Volunteers were needed to "get some chaps off the French coast." They were to sail first to Sheerness, the harbor on the Thames estuary.

Even though none of them could really imagine why all these small boats were being pressed into service, Rudi was immediately galvanized. "This must be urgent. Look, there are chaps from the City here still in their striped pants and their cuta-ways. Let's hurry and get our things together."

Hannah had a difficult time persuading the men that she needed to accompany them. "I handle boats well. I had my own, remember."

Dr. Zaleski said, "Who knows what we will run into in France? We don't know any details of this operation. Depending on its size, we may be dodging the *Luftwaffe*. It's not just a matter of a little sail across the Channel. There are U-boats and mines out there, Hannah."

She stood her ground. "If you are willing to risk it, then so am I. You will be glad of my help, I promise you. Rudi can tell you I don't fall apart in an emergency. And I have no family to worry about me."

For some reason, the last bit finally persuaded him. Amalia lent her a heavy pullover, woolen slacks, heavy socks, boots, an overcoat, and gloves. Hannah braided her hair and put it into a bun, pulling a stocking cap of Christian's over her head.

"Charming!" Rudi commented. She grinned. She couldn't imagine ever appearing before Samuel dressed in such a manly fashion. It felt wonderfully liberating.

The cook supplied them with a basket of tinned meats and baked beans, several loaves of bread and preserves, as well as fresh apricots and strawberries from the garden. Rudi rounded up some canteens and anything else he could find to fill with water. Dr. Zaleski put together a first aid kit containing sulfa and plenty of bandages

"Darling," Dr. Zaleski said to his wife, "any quilts or blankets you are willing to sacrifice would be much appreciated. I am certain it's beastly cold on that beach."

"How long will you be gone?" she asked and Hannah could hear the anxiety in her voice.

"A few days," the doctor said. "You are not to worry. You know I have nine lives, and Rudi is as agile as an alley cat. Hannah assures us she can take care of herself, and I am holding her to it."

In an amazingly short time, they were in the car with Amalia driving to the docks. Hannah turned her face away as the slim, elegant woman took her husband into a passionate embrace. "Take the very best care, darling. It could be dangerous," she heard the woman whisper.

Hannah was deeply grateful she wasn't saying good-bye to Rudi at this auspicious moment. It *could* be dangerous. But she was full of purpose.

She had never been on board *A New Day*, but it was a sleek yacht—mahogany with gleaming brass trim. Rudi unfurled the Union Jack he kept on board and placed it in a holder in the stern. She helped cast off and they eased out into the estuary among the traffic of other small craft presumably headed for

Sheerness Harbor, ahead on the Thames. Dr. Zaleski stood at the helm while Rudi searched below for their maps. It felt wonderful to be on the water again. Hannah had missed the sailboat she had left behind in Zurich.

When he came up out of the cabin, Rudi asked, "When do you suppose we'll find out where we're headed?"

"Don't we know?" asked Hannah. "Didn't they tell you anything?"

"No," the doctor said. "It seems it's all very hush-hush. My guess is that they want us out on the water before they tell us anything that could leak to the enemy. There must be twenty boats out here, and we're gaining as we go."

"Are you warm enough?" Rudi asked her.

"Lovely, thank you. I hope the fog continues all the way across the Channel into France." She loved the way the mist shrouded everything, making it seem as though they were in a fairy tale. What was making her so girlishly fanciful? The Stuka bombers were no part of anyone's fairy tale.

"We'll need it to protect us from the *Luftwaffe*," the doctor said, as though reading her mind.

She and Rudi huddled together on a bench to share their warmth, and despite the fact that she didn't know what danger was ahead, she felt content. They reached Sheerness at the mouth of the Thames close to four o'clock. There, the boat was inspected to judge its soundness. All around them, boats like theirs and even smaller ones were undergoing repairs. But the Zaleski yacht was pronounced fit for its mission. They were placed in the first convoy and instructed to proceed to Ramsgate, where they would top off their fuel tanks and receive the compass reading for their destination. If they had no compass, they would receive a map.

More curious than ever, Hannah watched as they moved out into the Strait of Dover among the company of their convoy of small boats. She thought about the probable strategy of the situation. All at once, it seemed perfectly clear to her, and the idea of it chased away her content. "What if France is falling?" she asked. "What if we are evacuating the British Expeditionary Force?"

"In little boats like this?" Rudi asked.

"Think about it. The destroyers and other big ships wouldn't be able to get close enough to the beaches to board the soldiers. All the small boats are needed to operate as a ferry service."

"But France can't be falling. They've scarcely begun to fight," Rudi said. "And surely, if they were evacuating they would do so from a decent dock."

"Nika thinks France was finished days ago," his stepfather said. "The Germans surprised them by breaking through the Ardennes. They didn't go near the Maginot Line, where the French have stood ready and waiting almost since the last war. If this is true the B.E.F. may have had to fall back upon the beaches where there are no docks. What Hannah says is actually within the realm of possibility. Think about it. The *Luftwaffe* will be bombing the ports to prevent British reinforcements and artillery from landing."

She watched as Rudi processed the thought. The implications were staggering. If they *were* evacuating the B.E.F., that meant that Britain was alone in her fight from this point on. And Hitler wasn't about to stop after such a stunning string of victories. He would try to invade.

At the thought, fear squeezed her heart until she was almost breathless. She sat down on a bench, hands shaking. *There was nowhere left to run.* They would have to make their stand. And in order to have a hope of defeating the German war machine, they needed the men in the B.E.F. This mission of theirs may have seemed thrown together and exceedingly odd, but the future of their adopted country depended upon its success.

Rudi whistled. "I hope you're wrong, Hannah, but I'm afraid that as unlikely as it sounds, it's the only thing that makes any sense." He paused to light a cigarette. "This seems a mad adventure. Only something that extraordinary would explain its madness."

Dr. Zaleski agreed and said, "Fotheringill always says the British are at their best when their backs are against the wall. This 'mad adventure' is an example of that, all right. It will certainly surprise the Germans. Who would ever anticipate such a move?" He gave a short laugh. "An armada of not only yachts, but everything else down to the smallest fishing boat! I think you're right, Hannah. We are to be the ferries." He offered her the helm. "Do you think you can steer? It may take all night to get to Ramsgate at this rate."

Hannah agreed to steer. She decided then and there that she liked Rudi's stepfather very much. But then, it said much about him that he was married to an unusual woman. According to Rudi, his mother had been a major force in Austrian politics before the *Anschluss* which had brought Austria under German dominion. Granted, she had worked through her husband, the Baron von Schoenenburg, but she was a brilliant, self-sufficient woman. Almost as soon as she arrived in England, shortly after Hannah had met her, she had brought a Nazi *agent provocateur* to justice. Though Amalia von Schoenenburg Zaleski was extremely feminine, she was not to be trifled with. She had even given Lord Halifax, the Foreign Secretary, a dressing down, telling him he did not understand Hitler. And she had been absolutely right.

The yacht was a sweet little craft. Of course, sailing was altogether different than driving a motorboat, but she was glad of something to do.

"Tell me about your father, Hannah," the doctor invited.

A pain flared in her chest, but she welcomed the opportunity nevertheless. "He was a very devout Jew, first and foremost. But next to that, he was a devoted and loving father. His way was quiet, but he always encouraged me in my goal to be a biochemist. When there were shootings in Zurich, he escorted me to and from the University rather than asking me to quit my studies." She thought for a few moments. "He was also very proud of my brother, who was a member of Parliament for the Socialist Party until it was disbanded." Her voice caught with too much emotion. How could she explain what she had lost? "I miss him terribly. I never would have guessed how much. He was my touchstone in many ways."

"I am so sorry, Hannah. Rudi also tells me your brother was shot by the Nazis and that your mother died recently. You have seen a lot of death these past few years."

She blinked back tears. "It helps a lot to be a guest of your family. You are very close, just like my family was. And thank you for bringing me on this mission. It is good to be engaged in something meaningful just now."

"I thought it might be. I know that's how Rudi's mother would feel, were she in your situation."

Rudi said, "You're right, Andrzej. When Father died, the fact that she had an important mission was her salvation."

"How about some dinner?" his stepfather asked. "Tinned ham and beans anyone?"

Defiance

{ 4 }

After they reached Ramsgate, they spent what was left of the night sitting in the fuel queue and then, when they were gassed up and had filled many gallon containers with surplus fuel, at anchor in the harbor. They were right on the Channel now. At the fuel stop, they had been given the compass point on the French coast they were to make for. Their convoy was to sortie at 23:00 hours that night. Once they had reached their destination, they were to pick up troops from the beach and ferry them to the destroyers and other large ships that would be anchored in as close as they could get. Then they were to return for more men, over and over, until all the troops were gone from the beach. It was just as Hannah had guessed.

Rudi checked the map and was surprised to find the compass point corresponded with a tourist beach—Dunkirk, just inside the French border with Belgium. "That explains the small boats. This place is no harbor."

"The Germans may already hold Calais," Andrzej said. "I'm afraid it's a measure of British desperation that they are staging anything like an evacuation at such a place. I suggest we all go below and get some sleep. Something tells me we are going to need it."

When they awoke, the harbor was swelled by at least four times the number of boats that had been there the night before. And more were still arriving. It continued to be foggy with a fine drizzle. The Channel appeared unusually calm to Rudi, who had made the crossing many times.

He could feel restlessness spread through the harbor. At noon, he and Hannah went ashore in the rubber dingy and bought oilskins to keep their clothes dry. They lunched at a crowded pub and listened to the rumors flying around. Apparently, they were part of the hastily conceived "Operation Dynamo." Gossip was rife about the condition of the French. Some surmised they had already surrendered unconditionally, leaving the British to fight alone. Others said there was fighting right on the beach at Dunkirk and that they would be sailing in the midst of it. However, everyone was eager to do their bit. The BBC blared in the pub, but there was silence about Operation Dynamo. There was also a complete lack of war news.

"You know," Rudi said, "as far as the Brits are concerned, it's an ordinary Sunday. They think Britain and France are taking care of Jerry across the Channel. If this is a major evacuation, it is going to be a big shock to the Brits at home. I wonder if there has ever been a British retreat this massive."

"Let's find a bakery and buy as many pastries and loaves of bread as we have coupons for," Hannah said. "I have money, and

I'm betting the men we pick up off that beach are going to be hungry."

Rudi agreed with the idea and they found a bakery near the edge of the port town which still had plenty. They returned to the boat with boxes of baked goods and their oilskins, allowing the doctor to go ashore and ring Rudi's mother.

"Saying my brother will be angry to have missed this is an understatement," Rudi reflected. "Only a few days left of his term."

"Speaking of joining up, I doubt we will return by the first of June, when you are supposed to report for duty," said Hannah. "Today is the twenty-ninth."

"I considered that," Rudi said. "But I think this is the more important thing right now. They need fighters so badly the RAF isn't going to turn me away for being a day or two late."

When she spoke again, Hannah's voice was very quiet. "You realize that the RAF and the Royal Navy are going to be the only thing between us and Germany if this is a total evacuation?"

"It's going to be a hell of a fight," Rudi said. He felt adrenaline shoot through him, setting his heart pounding. He was past ready to meet the Luftwaffe.

When the doctor returned, he reported that Rudi's mother had heard nothing on the BBC about the coming expedition.

"Did you tell her what we suspect?" Rudi wanted to know.

"Not on an open telephone line. Just that we would be gone a few days." He yawned and stretched. "Since we'll be on the water all night and are going to be busy when we reach our destination, I suggest you two nap while you can."

"What about you?" Hannah asked.

"I'll get some sleep when you wake up."

As Rudi lay in the bunk below, the boat gently rocking, he heard the tumult above as boaters worked off nerves by delivering playful insults and boasts about how they were going to slip in right under Jerry's nose. Hannah was asleep.

Had they made a mistake to bring her? What if they hit a mine? Or were torpedoed? What if there were strafed by the Luftwaffe? Had Andrzej brought his service weapon in the event that there was fighting on the beach? His stomach tightened at the idea of submitting Hannah to these dangers. Did she realize what might happen? Why had he not thought this through?

Strangely, he had perfect confidence that he and Andrzej would survive whatever danger existed. Well, perhaps not a torpedo. However, that would be over in an instant. His worry for Hannah would not allow him to sleep. Finally, he drifted off with the thought that she wouldn't thank him for being overprotective. Unlike him, Hannah was very good at thinking things through.

When they finally made their sortie, a hush fell over the community of boaters. All that was heard were their motors. The fog was dense, shrouding their lights to an eerie glow. Rudi felt intense excitement as the doctor carefully steered the course. Their convoy passed across the water like a silent organism. As she sat next to him on the bench, Hannah's eyes glowed with like excitement. Taking her hand, he put it between both of his and squeezed it. She squeezed back. For two hours they sat like this, until Rudi took over at the helm.

Rudi reckoned it would be about a six-hour journey, bringing them to the beach at 4 a.m., before the Luftwaffe had ascended to the skies—if indeed they could take off in this fog. In his mind he kept hearing the opening bars of Beethoven's Fifth Symphony: da da da DUM.

Any mines would appear to have been cleared, and their quiet approach apparently fooled any submarines. They were probably going to make it.

But what will happen once we get there?

Hannah stood up next to him, indicating she wished to take the helm. He gave it to her, but remained standing next to her, his hand on her shoulder. Rudi felt the need for contact in the eerie silence.

He fell to wondering what had happened to the French Army and the B.E.F. They had held the Germans at a stalemate for four years in the Great War. How had they had collapsed with such little resistance? Blitzkrieg must be devilishly effective. This wasn't a popular war in England or France, begun as it was over Poland. He didn't know the British well enough to know how successfully they would fight off an invasion, but their friend Anthony Fotheringill maintained that if it came to such a pass, the Brits would fight to the last man.

And Rudi did know Churchill personally. If Churchill could infuse his fighting spirit into his countrymen, they just might stand a chance. Rudi was certainly willing to do his part in the air. He knew what life under the Nazis was like, and he didn't want to endure it again. His entire adolescence had been spent in a kind of terror. At age ten, Chris had been nearly clubbed to death during a Nazi raid on their neighborhood Jewish bakery. His father had come close to death the first time in 1934 during an aborted Nazi coup when their leader, Chancellor Dolfuss, had been murdered. Andrzej had saved Father by getting him out of the chancellery into an ambulance.

During the hours that followed, Rudi found himself thinking of his father. The things he remembered about him now, over two years after his death, were his devotion to Rudi's mother and to his country. Father had not considered himself a gifted politician, but he had known he was an able advisor. He had stayed in the government, even during the dictatorship, because he wanted an independent Austria. Rudolf von Schoenenburg was virulently anti-Nazi, and for five years, he had trodden a complex path helping to lead a government that was balanced precariously between Socialists and Nazis, both of which danced to a foreign tune. In the end, he and the Austrian people had lost, and he had been killed for his efforts.

What if he were still alive? Rudi knew without a doubt that he would be on a boat that he owned, making for Dunkirk.

Instead, it was the doctor who came up behind him and Hannah, saying in a low tone. "I think we are almost to the beach. I can just make out firelight. Thanks for spelling me, but you had better give me the helm now."

It occurred to Rudi then to wonder if the operation had been kept so quiet that the men did not even know that they were coming. Their yacht was one of the first to approach the beach. Taking out a flashlight he blinked it on and off. Other boaters were starting to yell, "Ahoy, there!" "The navy is here!" and "Come aboard."

Rudi stripped off his oilskins and overcoat and Hannah did the same, ready to leap into the water if anyone needed help. Soon, a dark wave of men started wading toward their light in a steady stream. Rudi and Andrzej began to haul them on board while Hannah did her best to hold the yacht steady. After their initial greeting, they kept the operation as quiet as possible. Two of the men brought dogs with them who proceeded to shake themselves all over the now-slippery deck. When the yacht was full and they were obliged to set off, Andrzej promised those waiting in the water, "We'll be back."

He took over the helm while Rudi and Hannah passed out blankets, bread, pastries, and fresh water. The men were ravenously hungry and filthy, their uniforms ragged, their beards growing in, and they shook with the cold. Clearly they had been living in subhuman conditions hoping for rescue. But now, once they were away from the shore, they cheered and laughed, still keeping their voices suppressed, "Did we ever give Jerry the slip! Hip, hip, hooray! Hip, hip, hooray!" They clapped each other on the back and shook Rudi and Hannah's hands. "It's the eleventh hour," one man told Rudi. "The Jerrys are closing in on the beach. We're running low on ammunition and artillery. You are an answer to prayer."

"Keep a lookout for a ship," Andrzej told Hannah, who was standing at his side. "I haven't seen anything yet, and I don't even know where to look in this fog."

One of the troops spoke up. "They're over by the jetty. To the north."

A destroyer began to emerge from the mist on the other side of a pile of rocks that must be the jetty. Once they had circled it, Rudi watched as Andrzej queued up by the ladder behind other small rescue vessels. When their turn game, the troops scrambled from their boat up the ladder with shouts of, "Thank you, mates!" and "God bless you!"

With canteens on straps slung over his shoulders, Rudi climbed up the ladder last and filled up with fresh water from barrels by the ship's bulkhead. He shimmied down the ladder, his chest swelling with satisfaction as they turned off to get another boatload. The whole process had taken two hours.

"This is going to be slow work," said Hannah. "I'll get us something to eat."

As they made their way back to the beach, they heard the sound of artillery fire.

"Duck!" Andrzej commanded. "Low as you can. That artillery isn't close, I don't think, but they have some range."

Thus began their efforts to take men aboard under fire. Shrapnel hit the boat and Rudi winced as he heard the mahogany splitting. He only hoped they could remain in one piece until they had completed their mission. It was impossible to see through the fog how many men awaited them on the beach. Rudi wanted Hannah to go below deck, but she refused. On the third load, one of the troops recognized her as a woman.

"Miss or Ma'am, you are the bravest and most beautiful sight I've ever seen," he said humbly and managed to kiss her hand. Other troops were a bit more rowdy, but it was nothing she couldn't handle with a few acerbic words. Rudi's admiration for her pluck and stamina grew. Surely she was a woman in a million.

The three of them worked themselves past exhaustion under the constant threat of shell fire. As the sun rose, the air remained thick with fog, which was an unmitigated blessing. For as long as the weather remained like this, Rudi knew the Luftwaffe would be grounded.

But the random shelling took its toll around them. Nearby a neat little fishing boat was sunk. Zaleski called out to its crew who were flailing about in the shallow water.

"Come join us, and give us a hand," he called out. The New Day motored over next to the wreck and helped three men on board. It turned out they were Scottish businessmen from the City. The captain was badly wounded in the leg.

"Dr. Zaleski here will see to that," said Rudi. "I'm Rudi by the way, and this is Hannah."

"A lassie!" the little captain exclaimed. "Well, that is all well and fine. I'm McCormick and these other two are Gibson and McGill."

McGill spoke up. "I thought we only had weather like this in Scotland. Lord be praised, it's keeping the Stukas away."

Hannah helped McCormick down into the cabin where Rudi's stepfather was readying his impromptu surgery. The captain rested in one of the bunks, while the rest carried on until Rudi counted fourteen loads of soldiers had been hauled first to the destroyer, then a large commercial fishing trawler, followed by a commercial ferry.

They had worked themselves to exhaustion, plus there was always the worry that enemy fire might explode their reserve fuel tanks and blow up The New Day. The Scotsman helped move the tanks close to the gangplank that lead below where they were out of the direct line of fire.

The troops were innumerable, and Rudi could see that this was going to be the job of more than a day. The Scotsmen's irrepressible spirits buoyed Rudi's flagging energy, but finally Andrzej said, "We'll lose our edge if we don't rest. After this boatload, we'll take turns resting below. Hannah you go first."

As they drew close in to the beach, Rudi was stumbling with fatigue. He forgot to duck after a large explosion. In less than a second, shrapnel found his shoulder. He cursed loudly. Stifling the pain, he tried to pull the men aboard, but he was losing blood and strength quickly. Eventually, he felt himself slide to the deck underfoot.

"Oi! Mate at the helm!" he heard. "This bloke's down." Rudi felt a deeper blackness overpower him.

When he revived, he was below deck and the doctor was probing his wound. It hurt like the devil. "Stupid of me. I'm not likely to be much help now."

"You're going to be fine. I've managed to get the shrapnel removed and to stop the bleeding. I've got some sulfa here. Hopefully that'll prevent an infection."

"Did we get that last lot boarded?"

"Yes. We're at anchor now offshore. Here's some water. Drink plenty. You've lost a bit of blood. Hannah's making your dinner."

"I couldn't eat . . ."

"I'm the doctor. You will eat. Just as soon as I've bandaged you up here."

"I don't think we'll ever see the end of those troops. How many do you think there are?"

"It's hard to tell, but I'm guessing there must be thousands."

"It's like filling a reservoir with a teaspoon," Rudi said wearily.

"Now you're seeing the British at their best. We'll keep at it until the job is done. We took this last bunch to a commercial cruise ship moored out past the jetty. It looks like the navy has requisitioned everything that will float. The Scots are a big help. Captain McCormick is back on deck. They will spell us while we get some rest."

To his shame, Rudi remained below the whole next day fighting a fever while Hannah and Andrzej worked the operation and the Scots slept nosily on the remaining bunks and the deck below. Every time they off loaded another boatload, Hannah came down to check on him.

"Shirker," she said lightly, handing him a cup of water.

She changed his bandage once and was pleased to find that the wound looked good.

"You watch it up there," he said. "Where would we be if you got wounded, too?"

That night, his fever went down, and he insisted on manning the helm the following day. Andrzej pulled men aboard, then co-opted them to help him with the others. Hannah continued doling out blankets and water. They had long since run out of pastries, bread and fruit.

More merchant ships appeared off the coast, taking on as many men as they could before making off in the still-lingering fog. Several men came aboard wounded, and Andrzej bandaged them temporarily to stop the bleeding until they could get to sick bay on one of the big ships. Rudi managed to stay on his feet the entire day and slept heavily that night. His admiration for Hannah's stamina was immense, and even in the chaotic circumstances he felt his admiration as a comforting warmth in his chest. He watched, amused, as she warded off the amorous advances of yet another soldier.

On the fourth day, they took a load over to a destroyer by the jetty. An officer was using his megaphone to tell them, "We've evacuated as many men as we can. The skies are clearing, so we can expect the Stuka bombers to return. Make your way home. The defensive line has broken up as the rear guard has boarded, and the enemy is moving on to the beach. I repeat, make your way home. And jolly good work! Your lot has saved the British Army!"

After four days, had the teaspoons managed to fill the reservoir? As Rudi piloted the splintered craft back to London that night, Hannah and Andrzej slept heavily below. He had the strong sense of lightness and rightness. He suspected that they had all just participated in a miracle.

{ 5 }

When Anthony called at the Zaleski home on the evening of May 30, he found Amalia and Nika both in a state of nerves, seated in the drawing room and listening to the BBC on the wireless.

"Oh Anthony! Did you know? Andrzej and Rudi and Hannah . . . they took our yacht and they must be helping with the evacuation! They just confirmed on the wireless that that is what is taking place, though everyone had already begun to talk of seeing the poor soldiers in the streets."

He took a seat beside her. "I know little more than you. I did know an evacuation was planned, but it has proceeded willy-nilly. I certainly had no idea Andrzej and Rudi had gone. And Hannah?"

"It's true. She wouldn't let them leave without her. She has pluck, that woman. And you know I have confidence in all of them, but you must admit it's worrying to think of them in that little boat against the *Luftwaffe*! Surely the Germans are not letting them go without a fight. There must be artillery fire and bombing."

He did not know what to do except to take her hands in his and hold them tightly.

"If it helps, we've heard reports that the weather is foggy and the *Luftwaffe* are grounded. It is a tremendous thing they are doing, Amalia. There are roughly four hundred thousand troops stranded there, if you can imagine. Now, the estimates are that by tomorrow, the rear guard will be loaded and most of them will be coming home. It is a miracle of proportions we never could have imagined." He smiled at her gently. "The tales the returned soldiers are telling are incredible. Many of them owe their lives to the bravery of the men in the small boats who are picking them up on the beaches and carrying them out to the ships anchored further out. Men like yours."

"What is the news, Anthony?" Nika asked in French.

They switched to her language. Amalia said, "So they should be on their way home after tomorrow?"

Anthony let go of her hands and gave them a pat. "I cannot really say. I don't think anyone knows for sure. There is some talk in the F.O. of evacuating the French while they are at it."

They heard the front door bang shut as Christian came in. "I have been down at the pub talking to a couple of soldiers who just returned. They told me a fantastic story. They actually helped to make a pier out of lorries and artillery to help get the men off the beaches."

"Oh, darling," Amalia said. "What did they say about the gunfire? Are they firing on the small boats like ours?"

"I asked them," Christian said, his blue eyes alight. "They said the bombers have been grounded since yesterday when the small boats showed up. Bad weather. And there is shelling on the beaches, but the Jerrys are still being held off from actually coming onto the beach. It shouldn't be too bad for Andrzej and Rudi. I wish I were there!" He pulled both hands through his corn-colored hair in frustration, leaving it sticking up.

Anthony translated his news for Nika.

"How did they look?" Nika asked. "The soldiers?"

"Pretty rough," Chris said in his easy French. "They haven't been home yet. They were just barely off the train from Dover. Couldn't wait to get a drink and some food. It's easy to tell they've had a bad time of it. Mostly they talked about how confusing it was. Belgium surrendered, leaving their western flank completely exposed to the German offensive. And the French haven't been able to hold them on their end. It's been a scramble. Unbelievable."

"It sounds dreadful," his mother said.

Her son sat down, elbow on his knees, his hands clasped between them. "Anything to eat?"

Anthony learned at the office that the evacuation was concluded on June third. After ringing Amalia to tell her she could expect her husband home late that night, he then went down to the Thames to wait. For some reason, he felt personally responsible for his friends' safety. Andrzej, Rudi, and Hannah were not even citizens and they had risked their lives to bring home Anthony's fellow countrymen. He was desperately anxious that they should return unharmed.

Around 10 p.m. he saw badly battered boats begin to stray into Tough's boatyard. He was alarmed, not only at their condition, but at the condition of the men who disembarked. Some were bandaged; all were staggering with exhaustion. He didn't delay them, though he badly wanted an account. His anxiety grew. Very glad that he hadn't invited Amalia or Christian to watch with him, he tried to possess himself in patience. He forced himself to remember all the tight spots that he and Zaleski had been in together during the first Great War. The man had an uncanny ability to land on his feet. Hopefully, that had served him well this trip.

Anthony had a long wait. Zaleski's yacht, almost unrecognizable it was so damaged, puttered into its slip at 1 a.m. Bandaged and hollow-eyed, Rudi was at the helm.

"Ahoy, there!" Anthony called out.

"Ahoy!" came Rudi's reply. "Fotheringill?"

"It is I. You look a bit the worse for wear." Walking up to the yacht, he caught the line Rudi cast him and secured it to the cleat. Doing the same with the second line, he began to fear the worst when no one else appeared on deck.

Rudi disappeared below. Zaleski finally stumbled out. Bearded and disheveled, he looked to Anthony to have aged several years.

"Fotheringill! Good to see you, man!" he said. "You missed what you would have called a frightfully good show. Plenty of action. Didn't sleep much."

"It has all the makings of an epic," Anthony said. "What happened to Rudi?"

"He caught some shrapnel in his shoulder. He'll be all right."

At that moment, Hannah emerged, face smudged, hair in a tangle. Rudi followed, grinning from ear to ear. "Here's the heroine of your epic," he said.

"Mr. Fotheringill, how good of you to meet us," Hannah said.

"I brought the car. Let's get you home. The baroness is more than anxious to see you all." Breathing a deep sigh of relief, he shepherded them all to his Lagonda, parked on the Embankment.

𝒟

Amalia heard the car at 1:30 a.m. "They're here!" she said to Nika. Rousing Chris from the sofa, she ran to the door. Andrzej came up the walk and took her into his arms.

"I reek," he said. "No time for a bath the last little bit."

"I don't care, darling. Are you fit?"

"Perfectly. Just a bit tired. Rudi took some shrapnel in the shoulder, but he's all right."

She embraced her son, being careful of his wound, feeling his sturdy body beneath his overcoat—so much like Rudolf's, only taller. Blinking back tears of relief, she hugged Hannah as well. "You brave, brave woman. Thank you for making certain the men came out of that all right."

"She never stopped, *Mutti*," Rudi said. "She even nursed me when I was injured, in addition to everything else."

Amalia ushered them all in to the house, where Chris and Nika waited.

"Baths," she said. "Then bed."

"We could use something to eat," Rudi said.

"Baths first. And be sure you scrub your scalps. I feel sure you are covered in lice. I'll bring food upstairs myself."

She scurried into the kitchen where she and Nika scrambled eggs, an entire week's ration of fried bacon and tomatoes, and toasted thick pieces of bread. She put it all on two trays, along with apricot preserves, and jugs of milk. Together with Nika, she carried it upstairs.

They ate in her sitting room. Now that they were all clean, she could see the dark rings of exhaustion below their eyes and in the pallor of their faces. But they ate everything. Apparently they were too exhausted to speak.

"We have so much to tell you," Rudi said. "But bed first."

"Yes, I definitely agree," Amalia said.

When Andrzej had stretched out in their their bed, he instantly fell asleep. Curling up to him, she prayed her thanks over and over again, running her hands over his face, neck, and chest to reassure herself of his reality and well-being. She didn't even want to know how close she had come to losing him. If Rudi had been hit, that meant they had been under fire. Amalia shuddered, and put her head down over Andrzej's heart. She hadn't had much sleep herself, and could only drift off now, knowing that he was really here. That he was really all right.

Anthony rang in the morning to tell them that Churchill would be addressing Parliament that evening. "I think this speech will be memorable. I would encourage you all to get to the gallery in good time to hear it. You need to know just what you have been part of."

The Times gave a rough idea: About a quarter of a million men had been rescued! This was ten times the amount that the War Cabinet had anticipated could be evacuated. Amalia could hardly believe that in that short of a time, with no advanced planning, such huge numbers of men had been taken off the beaches. It was further estimated that a third of the number left the beaches in small boats like theirs.

No wonder her family was so exhausted. She wondered if they even knew what they had accomplished.

When Andrzej, Rudi, and Hannah woke around the noon hour, she saw that they were well-fed using all the rations for the meals they had missed while on their mission.

She told them of estimates in *The Times.* "Had you any idea it was such a huge effort?"

Andrzej answered, "Frankly, no. Rudi said it was like filling a reservoir using a teaspoon. That's exactly what it felt like. We worked day and night, scarcely stopping, but there were always more men. And dogs, if you can believe it."

Rudi touted his stepfather's and Hannah's bravery and stamina, especially during the period when he lay below, recovering.

"Anthony rang this morning. The Prime Minister is to speak to Parliament this evening," Amalia said. "I feel we must go early to get seats in the gallery."

Chris added, "I have been out to the shops this morning. There is near delirium in the streets. People are over the moon about your heroics. They are stopping to talk to other Londoners in the street who they don't even know. People never do that here!"

"I would like to hear Mr. Churchill," said Andrzej.

That afternoon, they drove to the Parliament building. People clogged the streets. As Chris had said, it was very unlike London. Instead of people scurrying along, they were stopped in groups, surrounding the soldiers, embracing them, and hauling them into pubs.

Rudi was glad they were early, for they got some of the last seats in the gallery. The Members filed in after dinner, clapping one another on the shoulder, speaking in congratulatory phrases. Gradually, they assumed their places on the green leather benches. It was clear everyone felt a great deal of pride in what was being referred to as "The Miracle of Dunkirk."

Mr. Churchill strode into the House Chamber, his cigar in his mouth, a sheaf of notes in his hand. Rudi felt great awe and even affection for the man. He and his family had been the Churchills' guest at Chartwell for close to a month after their arrival in England. In Rudi's view, the man was every inch a man to believe in and to be relied upon. He and only he had foreseen the damage that Hitler would wreck upon Europe.

He began to speak about the horrible prospect that had been before them only a week before: "The whole root and brain and core of the British Army on which and around which we were to build, the great British armies, in the later years of the war, seemed about to perish upon the field or to be led into an ignominious and starving captivity."

Then he spoke of the efforts which had changed the course of the army's history: "Suddenly the scene has cleared, the crash and thunder has for the moment—but only for the moment— died away. A miracle of deliverance, achieved by valor, by perseverance, by perfect discipline, by faultless service, by resource, by skill, by unconquerable fidelity is manifest to us all."

A warm glow rose in Rudi's breast, and he sought Hannah's hand and squeezed it. He saw tears in his mother's eyes, and then they were falling down her cheeks. Mr. Churchill had a remarkable turn of phrase. The house rang with the numbers of the rescued which he gave, taking Rudi's breath away—"Over 335,000 men, French and British."

But the Prime Minister was far from finished. He next uttered a warning: "We must be very careful not to assign to this deliverance the attributes of a victory. Wars are not won by evacuations . . ." He spoke of the role of the RAF in the effort, he spoke of the losses of the army in France—30,000 men at last count—and the task that lay before them.

Then he uttered words which Rudi knew he would never forget. Words that would ring in his ears as he flew his Spitfire over the Channel: "Even though large tracts of Europe and many old and famous states have fallen or may fall into the grip of the Gestapo and all the odious apparatus of Nazi rule, we shall not flag or fail. We shall go on to the end, we shall fight in France, we shall fight on the sea and oceans, we shall fight with growing confidence and growing strength in the air, we shall defend our Island, whatever the cost may be, we shall fight on the beaches, we shall fight on the landing grounds, we shall fight in the fields and in the streets, we shall fight in the hills, we shall never surrender . . ."

How great it was to hear the stirring words of a leader finally willing to take a stand against their enemy! If only Rudi's father could have lived to hear them. Rudi pledged to stand in his place. He put his arm around his mother's waist and pulled her to his side. Tears streamed down her cheeks. "We are going to win this war, *Mutti.* We are going to win it!"

{ 6 }

When Anthony went to the Foreign Office the day after
Churchill's Dunkirk speech, he expected the mood to be lighter
than the atmosphere of heavy tension they had lived with for the
past weeks. His friend, Nigel Reston, met him in the hall on the
way to his office.

"The news isn't good from France," Nigel said.

"Come into my office," Anthony invited.

They sat down on his leather wing backed chairs and simul-
taneously began to fill their pipes. "What have you heard?" he
asked.

"Apparently, now that our chaps are gone, the French are
caving in right and left. I spoke to Halifax this morning. He'd
been with the PM. In spite of Churchill's attempts to reassure
the French that we are still their ally, they are feeling bitter.
He's promised to send back some of the troops we took off the
beach after they've had a shave and a brush up, but to me that

seems like a needless sacrifice." Reston lit his tobacco and drew on his pipe. "What do you think?"

"I'm glad the decision isn't mine to make. When France falls, maybe our conscience will be a bit more clear, but those men may end up prisoners or worse."

"Exactly." Reston stood up and went to the window, his stance rigid. Turning around, he said, "Just between the two of us, do you think Jerry has us beaten?"

Anthony looked at his friend in surprise. "Good heavens, no. We haven't even begun to fight."

"I know that's the official line, but don't you think it's a bit naïve?" Reston asked, irritation marking his voice.

"Difficult, perhaps. Beating off an invasion will require not only stamina and nerve, but a bit of luck. However, I haven't a doubt we can pull it off. After the Dunkirk miracle, the people are primed to stand firm and start fighting. Up until now the war hasn't seemed real to them."

Reston beat his index finger on the bowl of his pipe. "What do you suppose Churchill has up his sleeve?"

"No secret weapon. I think any Brit should be able to guess his program: stand firm and let the RAF gain air mastery over the Channel. Keep the Royal Navy in the fight, employing it to blockade the coast. Use every possible expedient to increase our artillery production. Station the army at all possible invasion points," Anthony said. "You know, the Jerrys haven't thought this through. Granted, they've had nothing but success so far, but Britain is a different case altogether. Intelligence says they have no landing craft. This island isn't that easy to take, Reston. Plus, we have the resources of the Empire."

His friend rose. "I wish I had your optimism."

G.G. Vandagriff

"You had better have a go at cultivating some," Anthony said sharply. "What's eating you, Reston?"

"It should be obvious. Hitler's no lunatic. He's a genius. He's leveled Northern Europe as though it were armed with paper soldiers. Contrary to your thinking, I suppose him to have the details of an invasion completely thought out."

Anthony was truly surprised by his friend's prognosis. Reston had always shown himself to be steady and solid. "It sounds like you've been listening to German propaganda. The reason Jerry has been so successful is simply because our government, up 'til now, has avoided a real commitment to war. We could have defeated them in '38 when they went after Czechoslovakia, but Chamberlain chose appeasement. Now we have no choice but to fight for our very life. This is a different country than it was a week ago."

"Too little, too late," said Reston as he walked out of the office.

Anthony shook his head, drummed his fingers on the desktop for a moment, then looked at the piles of memoranda he needed to sift through. War was causing chaos in the Foreign Office. Relations with Italy were strained, not to mention the whole mess with the Soviet Union caused by their violation of Poland's sovereignty.

After working long hours all through the Dunkirk situation, he needed a break. Part of him wanted to ring Nika to ask her to go out for coffee. But memories of Madge held him back, painful and dark.

The train journey home seemed as though it would never end. The pain in his leg was next to intolerable. They had run out of morphine at his field hospital. He longed to see Madge, to have the cool comfort of her hand caressing his brow. He had missed her terribly in the trenches. A small framed portrait of her in a black velvet evening gown was stowed next to his razor even now. Her lavender eyes appeared light in the black and white portrait, while her dark hair was swept up in an elegant twist. Her gamine face looked out at him with a playful smile, despite the serious nature of the occasion. One was not supposed to smile for photographs, but Madge couldn't hold a smile back for toffee.

And then there was his daughter Sonia to look forward to. He had no idea what to expect there. He had never had a child before.

When they finally arrived in London, his stretcher was carried off the train. Madge was there, wearing a hat with feathers, holding an infant in a trailing mass of blankets. She rode in the ambulance with him to the hospital and he saw his daughter for the first time. She was incredibly tiny, with a nose no bigger than a button. How could he have sired such a beautiful, perfect creature? Madge was full of gossip, rattling on in the way she had. He couldn't remember a word. All he could think of was the piercing pain in his leg.

At the hospital, they told her to come back for visiting hours that afternoon. He hoped by then that the morphine would have kicked in.

She didn't come that afternoon. In fact, she didn't come for three more days. Had she been struck by an automobile? Was something wrong with Sonia? He fretted the days away.

When she came finally, it was without the baby and she offered no explanations. He was sitting up in a wheel-chair out on a small terrace overlooking a pleasant garden, thinking how grateful he was to be away from the mud and stink of the *trenches. The pain in his leg, thanks to the morphine, had less-ened to a dull throbbing.*

A nurse showed Madge out to the terrace.

"... he is a very good patient. I will show you how to care for the surgery site. He should be ready to go home in a couple of days."

Madge's smile was very uncertain as she drew close to him. She sat on a low brick wall rather than in the chair next to him.

"Would you mind very much, Anthony, dear, if we hired a live-in nurse to care for your leg? I don't think I can quite man-age it with Sonia and everything."

"Of course not," he said. "Whatever you think best. I wouldn't want to be a burden."

And he wasn't. Madge was not even home when he got there, transported again by ambulance. As the days went by, she was there less and less. Sonia was continually in the nursery with her nanny. He scarcely saw either of them.

A black despair settled on him as he realized that Madge couldn't even look him in the eye on the rare moments when they were together. He had a hard time convincing himself that he was lucky to be alive, sitting in the garden in his wheelchair, day after day. Hiring workmen through his butler, he oversaw the construction of a koi pond with a Chinese bridge over it which he had designed, filling in the empty hours. He looked for signs of hope, but found none.

Eventually, Zaleski came home on leave. He came to stay with Anthony, as his home was behind enemy lines in Poland. They played a lot of chess and talked late into the evenings, smoking their pipes together. The friendship of that remarkable man was the glue he needed to put his life back together. Zaleski was an optimist, even in the dark hours. He talked about Amalia during those times. His version of love was something beyond Anthony's experience.

Then came the day Anthony was fitted with his prosthesis. Madge was instructed how to take it off and put it back on. Tears running down her face, she refused to touch it.

That night, she came to him in his study. "Anthony, I'm no good at this sort of thing. We might as well face it. It makes me physically ill. I'm taking Sonia and going home to my parents."

Rejection sliced through him like a razor. The pain remained for years, and would have seriously hampered his recuperation had not so many other men suffered similarly. Some of their wives stayed with them. Some of them left as Madge had done.

Last May, after twenty years, she filed for divorce. She was now remarried to one Viscount Bassington, the wealthy scion of a noble family in Wiltshire.

Anthony stared at the telephone on his desk, wondering if he could ever let another woman into his life. Wondering if there was any chance he could experience the kind of love the Zaleskis so clearly had. He was battered and scarred, both mentally and physically.

Nika knows no one but Andrzej and Amalia. She has been through an exceedingly rough time. There is nothing wrong with asking her out for coffee. She probably won't even accept.

Picking up the instrument, he rang the Zaleski household and asked to speak with Nika.

She answered a bit breathlessly. "'ello?"

He greeted her in French and asked if she would meet him for coffee at The American Café in Piccadilly Circus. She agreed readily. After giving her the address for the taxi driver, he hung up, grabbed his hat, trench coat, and umbrella, and hustled down to the street, where he hailed a cab.

Arriving at the spot which he always thought of as the heart-beat of London, he strolled into the popular café and managed to snag a table near the back. When Nika came through a few moments later, he raised his umbrella and she came toward him.

Dressed in an electric blue suit over a black blouse which suited her dark beauty, Nika possessed the effortless elegance, that *je ne sais quoi* of a Frenchwoman, though she was Polish. She probably saw him as ancient and doddering, but Anthony's heart lifted at the sight of her. He had done very well without female companionship for a long time now, so what was it about this woman that stirred his blood and made him think things could be different?

Her courage combined with that sense of vulnerability, perhaps? He really couldn't put his finger on it.

Joining him, she said, "Thank you for ringing me. The Zaleskis are wonderful hosts, but I am certain they are glad to have me out of the house for a bit."

"I am sure you exaggerate. What would you like? Coffee? Tea? A sticky bun?"

"Do they still have them here? I would adore a sticky bun. I brought my ration book. And coffee with cream, please."

Anthony gave their order to the waitress who had suddenly materialized.

"I thought you would appreciate hearing about my conversation with my sister in person," he said.

"Oh? So you have spoken with her?"

"Yes. She would like to know what languages you speak. You are to send her a résumé." He pulled a paper from his inside breast pocket. "Here is her address. Come to think of it, you actually might want to make a day trip to Oxford to deliver it yourself. It's quite convenient by train. Then you could just take a taxi to Somerville College and ask the porter for Professor Fotheringill."

"I didn't give the language issue a thought," Nika admitted with a frown. "But my English is weak."

"My sister speaks very good French. You can thrash things out with her. Perhaps you can teach in French. Facility with the language is a requirement for entrance to Somerville, apparently."

Their coffee arrived, and they busied themselves with adding cream and sugar. Anthony watched as Nika surveyed their surroundings. The café was very *avant garde* in black and white, with chromium Art Deco fixtures and posters of American film stars.

"This is all a world away from the war," she said.

"Not for long, I expect."

"You are right." She looked away from him. "I am not very brave, Anthony. In fact, I am frightened."

A silence fell between them as Anthony watched Nika stir her coffee, her eyes full of pain. He said, "I have never been to Warsaw. Tell me about your life there."

She gave a gusty sigh and he instantly regretted his question. He was clutching at topics to discuss, but why hadn't he thought a bit before opening his mouth?

"The city is not as big as London, of course, but it was very busy and elegant in its own way. I lived with my parents in a home very similar to the Zaleskis'. My father was a Count, but he was also an architect. Rather a lot of building went on in Warsaw between the last war and this."

"I'm sorry if this is too painful," he said. He stifled an impulse to reach across the table for her hand.

"It is, rather. Let's talk about you, instead." She gave a smile, but it looked as though she had just tasted something bitter. "How is it you have never married?"

He felt the question like a blow. *So she didn't know.* "I was married," he said. "I have a daughter, as a matter of fact."

"Your wife died? I am sorry." Her forehead contracted in an expression of concern.

Needing to occupy his hands now that he had finished his coffee, he drew his pipe out of his pocket. "She left me."

"Oh!" A flush climbed up her cheeks.

"You might as well have the full story," he said, looking up from his tobacco pouch. She was sitting straight as a statue. "Yes. I am divorced. After twenty years of living apart, Madge decided she wanted to marry again."

She said nothing. After a moment, she began to tear her sticky bun apart.

"You see I was badly wounded in the last war. I lost the lower part of my right leg. She never adjusted. I can't really blame her."

Nika compressed her lips. "That is horrible. Not that you lost your leg . . . I mean, of course that is horrible . . . but how could she leave you for such a reason? And divorce! That is so cruel. So final."

"I knew you wouldn't like it. "

"You know then that I am Roman Catholic?"

"I supposed you were."

She grimaced. "I have a bit of a past, myself," she said. "Tearing what was left of her pastry into tiny bits, she continued, "My husband was in a motor accident. He was killed."

This time, Anthony could not ignore his impulse. He reached across the table for her hand. It was small and soft in his. Before he realized it, he was caressing it with his thumb. "How rotten for you." Was there any sorrow this woman had escaped?

She raised her chin. "It was rotten, but I survived it. It happened a long time ago. Ten years, to be exact."

He squeezed her hand. "And now you have lost both parents and your brother. You are in a foreign country where you are not comfortable with the language, and there is a war on. I think you are incredibly brave."

"Thank you. You are wonderfully kind." She held his hand tightly, her eyes soft with sorrow.

The words warmed him through.

Tears welled in her eyes, and she let go of his hand to wipe them with her napkin. "I feel like taking a brisk walk. Will that bother your leg?"

"No. That sounds just the thing." He knocked out the pipe he had never lit, laid some pound notes on the table and stood. Guiding her with a hand at the small of her back, he walked her through tables filled with people engrossed in conversation and out into the petrol-fumed air of Piccadilly.

"You must take a mental photograph of this day," Nika said, looking around her at the bustling shops, theaters, and restaurants. "When the *Blitzkrieg* comes, London will no longer look like this."

Her large eyes appeared haunted. Anthony could hardly bear to think of what memories she must carry from Warsaw. "I wish I could take away your suffering, your terrible memories."

"No one can," she said, tucking a hand inside his elbow. She began walking.

"I have been telling myself for years not to look back, but to look to the future," he said. "It's easier said than done, but perhaps we should give it a try."

"How does one do that in war time?"

"Well for one thing, you're not looking ahead to another defeat. We may get bombed, but we will prevail in the end. Hitler will not take this Island."

"You sound very certain."

"I've been through a war. I'm not naïve. I just know my people. Now that they've made up their minds to fight, things are going to be different. As I was telling my co-worker this morning, this is a different country than it was last week. I shall translate Churchill's speech to the House of Commons last night for you. You will then see what we are made of."

He stopped at a newsstand and bought a paper. Hailing a taxi, he told the driver to take him to Laurel House, the Zaleskis' home. He began to translate the speech from the newspaper as they rode.

When they stopped before the Mayfair dwelling, Nika commented, "Brave words. We were full of brave words in Poland, too."

{ 7 }

Nika didn't know why she resisted Anthony's attempts to bring her a measure of peace. She only knew how she felt—like a rag doll that had been violently ripped apart, her stuffing bursting from the seams, her head cockeyed on her shoulders.

And she was haunted. Every night, as she tried to sleep, she heard the eerie scream of the Stuka dive bombers and was haunted by visions of bodies blown to bits. For some reason, the worst memory was the dead horses lying everywhere crawling with maggots—possibly because they seemed more real. The idea of living through another *Blitzkrieg* simply made her want to walk into the river and end it all.

Did he know what a coward she was? As they pulled up before The Laurels, she said, "Thank you for the coffee. And for trying to cheer me. I think I must have something to do. Without anything to occupy my mind, I am far too apt to dwell on my fears, especially at night."

"I know I cannot possibly imagine what you have been through. But I am trying to understand," he said. After asking the driver to wait, he walked around and opened her door. "I'll ring my sister from inside, if you like. We can see if she would be able to visit with you tomorrow. Just seeing Oxford would have a soothing effect on you, I think. It is ancient and beautiful and one has the feeling that it will go on and on forever."

Before going inside, she stood on the stoop and looked at him. He was very nice to look at with his kind blue eyes, regular features, sandy blond hair, and square cleft chin exactly like Cary Grant's. "Why are you being so kind to me?" she asked.

He put a comforting hand on her shoulder. "I have been through one terrible war already. I know what hell it can wreck on one's mind and heart. It pushes one to the edge of hopelessness. But without hope, one can't go on. I am trying to help you to see that there is reason to hope."

She bowed her head under his intense gaze. He really believed what he was saying. Opening the door, Nika said, "I would like to see Oxford and meet your sister."

"Splendid. I'll ring her now, and we'll arrange it. Then I'm afraid I must get back to the office." He followed her inside the house.

Professor Irene Fotheringill said she would be very happy to lunch with Nika the next day. She would meet her at The Mitre on the High Street at one o'clock. After they ate, she would have time to take Nika on a tour of the colleges.

Anthony gave her a heartwarming smile as he stood ready to go.

"Thank you for everything," she said.

"I'll ring you tomorrow evening to see how your day went," he promised.

A sudden impulse gripped her and, standing on her tip-toes, she kissed him on the cheek. "You are more than kind. Splendid, in fact."

Lifting his hat, he grinned, looking years younger. "Cheerio!"

When he disappeared through the door, she stood in the vestibule looking after him.

Her heart was beating a little faster, and she felt the gray fog that shrouded her mind lift a tiny bit.

Hannah returned to The Laurels after signing up for the WAAFs. All the time, she carried with her a special letter of commendation from Mr. Churchill telling of valuable services to His Majesty's Government, overriding any attempt to detain her as an Austrian national expressly at his request. She knew the entire von Schoenenburg family carried similar documents. It had certainly come in handy when she made her application.

Though she was still a bit tired from the Dunkirk adventure, her spirits were optimistic. She was to be stationed at Uxbridge in southeast England. Since Dover was the closest port to France, she and everyone else supposed that southeastern port would receive the worst of the bombing when it came. The Channel was at its narrowest at that point, so it only made sense that the *Luftwaffe* would engage the fighters closest to the area where they could take off.

She found Rudi at loose ends, having been granted leave for one more week until his shoulder healed.

"We must go out and celebrate your induction into the WAAFs," he said. "Lunch at the Savoy, I think. We will make this a day to remember."

Hannah laughed, her spirits soaring. Rudi looked so devil-may-care handsome with his sling worn over the brown tweed jacket that exactly matched his eyes. His auburn hair was adorably mussed. "Let's! I must change my clothes. You, too. A tweed jacket will never do for the Savoy."

She donned a chic white suit that flared at the knees, with a navy and white polka-dotted neck scarf. Since she was reporting for duty in two days, she wanted to grab every last minute of time with Rudi and make it memorable.

When he saw her, Rudi's eyes lit, and she was pleased. Taking her hand, he kissed it. "I shall have to be careful not to stray from your side or someone will steal you away."

"Never," she said. "You look very elegant, yourself." Rudi wore a dark cutaway jacket with a gray and black striped cravat. Her heart sped up. Samuel was more handsome, but next to this man he would be short and spare. Rudi was every inch the Baron von Schoenenburg with his patrician nose and large, square shoulders.

The Savoy Grill was full of men in uniform, and even at this noon hour a band played on the dais and there was dancing. The *maître d'* seated Rudi and Hannah at one of the round tables and handed them large, heavy menus.

"I haven't forgotten that you love to dance," he said. "After we order, I plan to take you to the floor."

"Can you do the Swing?" she asked.

"Of course. Dancing the Swing is an essential part of the modern-day baron's repertoire. Can you do the Tango?"

"You must teach me," she said with a laugh. "I would dearly love to tango with you. It looks so dramatic in the films."

Rudi ordered a bottle of wine and a bowl of mussels as an appetizer. Hannah felt an effervescence of spirits she hadn't known in months. Whenever thoughts of Samuel intruded, she told herself that her fiancé and marriage were for the future. Rudi was for now. All too soon, he would be over the Channel in his Spitfire, challenging the *Luftwaffe.* Who knew what would happen then? She blamed this recklessness she was feeling on the unknowns in their future.

After drinking a glass of wine, Rudi removed his sling. "I don't need this for dancing."

"But won't it jar your arm?"

"I'm Viennese. I could dance with one arm missing if I had to."

So they danced an energetic Swing. Rudi was indeed very good, which didn't surprise her. Her spirits flew even higher as he spun her around. She promised herself that she would remember this moment in time when they were both alive with such happiness.

As Rudi taught her the Tango and she looked straight into his eyes, Hannah felt a dangerous pull. Everything inside her was tuned to him. Though exaggerated, all their moves were natural and right. And she could read Rudi's feelings for her in his eyes and in his touch, commanding her with their own brand of tenderness.

Is this more than a good time?

Compared to the solid cords that bound her to Rudi, her relationship with Samuel seemed to be composed of fragile threads.

As they left the dance floor, she realized that even married to Samuel, she would feel a horrible loss if Rudi were not alive somewhere in the world. When they returned to their table, she drank off an entire glass of wine. Facing him, she said, "Rudi, promise me you'll take care."

He gave her a brief, one-sided smile. "I am a fighter pilot. That will be the last thing on my mind."

"I couldn't bear to lose you," she said, tears starting to her eyes.

He took her chin in his hand. "What's this? You're engaged to be married to someone else. You have *chosen* to lose me."

Looking him straight in the eye, she said, "You know how I feel about you. You must. I am marrying Samuel because it is what Papa wanted."

He took her hands. "I don't think you have thought this through properly. Marrying Samuel isn't just a single act. It's a lifelong commitment. I will not be your lover, Hannah. For me, it's all or nothing."

Taking her lower lip between her teeth, she looked down. Of course that was the way Rudi felt. He was honorable to the nth degree. Manufacturing a smile, she said, "What are we doing talking about this now? We are here to have a good time! Look, here comes your fish."

Hours later, when they returned to The Laurels, Simms informed her that a Mr. Weissman was awaiting her in the morning room.

Rudi looked a question at her and her heart dropped into her middle. Samuel! What was he doing here?

"It's Samuel," she told Rudi, her voice sounding grim even to her own ears. "Come, let me introduce you."

Rudi studied her for a moment, but she was unable to read his expression. Finally, he said, "All right."

Standing before the closed door to the morning room, Hannah took a deep breath. She opened the door into the coral-colored room.

"Hello, Samuel," she said as her fiancé rose.

He looked at her without a smile. "Hannah. And this must be von Schoenenburg?"

"Yes. Rudi, please meet my fiancé, Samuel Weissman. Samuel, this is the Baron Rudolf von Schoenenburg."

Rudi walked forward, his hand extended, "Mr. Weissman."

"Baron," Samuel said, shaking his hand.

"I don't use my title here," Rudi said.

She couldn't help comparing the stature of the two men. Rudi—straight and tall and alive. Samuel, built on a smaller scale looked like a vanilla-flavored dreamer.

"Was it your idea to take Hannah with you on that insane mission to Dunkirk?" he asked, his face stiff with what she realized was anger.

Why must he be so difficult? Hannah wondered.

"I don't tell Hannah what and what not to do," Rudi replied. "She has been deciding things for herself for a long time."

"Samuel, you are out of line," Hannah said. "I begged Rudi's stepfather to take me and he agreed."

Her fiancé ignored her speech, focusing on Rudi's sling. "You were wounded, I presume."

Rudi only nodded.

"Samuel, you are being absurd. I have returned safely." She barely kept her temper in check. She had never seen this side of her betrothed, but to be fair, he had never seen her reckless side, either.

"You put your life at risk unnecessarily," he maintained.

"It wasn't unnecessary. As it turned out Dr. Zaleski couldn't have managed without me once Rudi was wounded. And even before he was wounded, it was a job for three people." She put her hands on her hips. "I decide what risks I take with my life. It is *my life!*"

Samuel's eyes ignited with anger. She stood up straighter.

"You didn't tell me you were coming to London to see your old beau."

"Rudi is my best friend in the world. I was bereft after Papa died. My family was gone. The von Schoenenburg family has made me welcome under difficult circumstances before. I chose to come to be with them, not just Rudi."

"I would be glad of a word alone, Hannah, if the baron will excuse us."

To her surprise, Rudi kissed her forehead, bowed his head stiffly in Samuel's direction, and left without a word.

Hannah took a seat in a wing chair as far from Samuel as possible.

"That man is in love with you."

Lifting her chin, Hannah said nothing.

"Do you love him?" her fiancé demanded.

"I don't know," she answered. "But it is immaterial because I won't marry him. I am engaged to marry you, and I will honor that engagement."

"Because of your father. I am not as ignorant as you think, Hannah." His eyes pierced hers with their sadness.

"Rudi's and my friendship will come to a natural close when he joins his RAF unit in a week. The day after tomorrow, I will report to the WAAFs. We have been kicking up our heels one last time."

Samuel sneered at her. "You plan to take him for a lover, don't you?"

"Definitely not." Guilt shot through her. If Rudi had been willing, would she be able to make this promise?

"Can you promise me that? That you will be faithful to me once we are married?"

"Yes. If I wanted to marry Rudi, I would, Samuel. I am going to marry you, unless you continue to carry on like a jealous fool."

His whole body relaxed and he dropped onto the ivory sofa, covering his face with his hands. "I am sorry, Hannah. Your letter made me sick with horror over what might have happened to you. And then you walked in here with that . . . that baron . . . and I saw red."

Hannah couldn't bring herself to go to him. He didn't belong in this part of her life. All the joy she had felt that day was obscured like the sun dipping behind a cloud. It was suddenly very clear that living without Rudi in her life was going to be like cutting out a vital organ. Part of her would continue to live, but she would be forever emotionally handicapped. Life would never be what it could have been. Now that her anger was cooling, she could see that she needed to be straight with Samuel.

"Rudi is obviously not a Jew. Papa did not approve of him."

"I see." The anger had gone, but Samuel looked far from happy. "Will you promise me not to see him again once you have left this house?"

Hannah felt a spurt of panic at the idea. "We are not married yet, Samuel."

"Is he the reason you have postponed the wedding, then? The reason you wanted to join the WAAFs?"

Bowing her head, she fidgeted with the scarf around her neck. "I . . . I don't know."

Samuel stood, and Hannah could feel his weariness. "I suggest you figure things out, my dear. I don't intend to marry someone who is in love with another man, even if she won't marry him."

Hannah didn't know what her response should be. "I will come to Oxford when I have leave, Samuel. We can talk about it then. I will have had time to get used to my feelings and I hope I will understand them better."

Samuel moved to the door. "As always, you are honest. I will wait to hear from you then."

After he left, Hannah remained where she was. Tears started down her cheeks. It was clear to her that she could not imagine life without Rudi. What was she going to do with these feelings?

{ 8 }

Though Rudi was anxious to talk with Hannah after her visit with Samuel, she seemed to be avoiding him. She had dinner in her room, giving the excuse of a headache. The following day, she was already out of the house when he came down to breakfast.

"She said she had shopping to do," his mother told him as he helped himself to eggs and toast from the sideboard. "Did she seem upset?" Rudi asked.

"No, she was very pleasant, though she only had a boiled egg and seemed in a bit of a hurry. Is something wrong?"

Rudi shrugged. "Her fiancé paid her a visit yesterday. He wasn't pleased about her adventure at Dunkirk."

"I can't blame him for that," his mother said. "But what little I know of Hannah leads me to believe that she is her own woman."

"Just like you are," Rudi said with a grin. "She has joined the WAAFs, you know."

"Good for her. She will be splendid."

The doctor entered the breakfast room and helped himself to a muffin and a cup of coffee. "Rudi, how is your shoulder?" he asked.

"Well enough. I can move it fairly well now."

"You are very fortunate that the joint wasn't shattered. That would have been the end of your career in the RAF," the doctor said. "Do you think you might feel well enough to help Christian and me put up the Anderson shelter in the back garden?"

"What is involved?"

"It's a prefabricated metal hut, but we need to dig a bit in the ground for a good foundation, and then the whole thing must be covered with sandbags."

"I think that may be beyond Rudi just now," his mother said, her brow furrowed with concern.

"Digging may be a bit much," Rudi said. "But I can haul sandbags and help you fit out the shelter. I'm glad you're taking these precautions, but wouldn't it be a better idea to leave London for the countryside?"

"We are working at the hospital," his mother said. "Fighter pilots who are badly injured near Dover are being brought there. And if London is bombed, we will be full to overflowing, I am sure."

He covered his mother's hand with his own. "As usual, you are in the thick of things." Rising from the table, he said, "I'm off to do some shopping of my own. I won't be gone long. Send Chris to find me somewhere in the house when you are ready for my help in the garden."

The doctor nodded, and Rudi left the room, went downstairs, and out into the morning. It was a perfect June day as he sauntered down the street looking for a cab to take him to Bond Street.

Once there, he strolled by the window displays in the jeweler's shops. Although he intended to emerge alive from this war, he would be a fool if he didn't take the other outcome into consideration. He wanted Hannah to have something from him to remember him by. Something simple but elegant. Spying just what he wanted in the window of the third jeweler, he entered the shop and asked to see it.

The shop assistant brought the diamond solitaire pendant out for him to view.

"It is two carats. A respectable size for this type of necklace. The chain and setting are eighteen carat gold," the man told him.

Rudi held the piece in his palm and walked over to the window where the sun leant it some sparkle. He wished it could be a ring signifying their engagement, but the occasion for that might never arise.

"I'll take it," he said after negotiating the price. "Please wrap it as a gift."

He returned home, whistling.

Hannah joined the family for dinner that evening, but her mood was solemn and she didn't enter the conversation. Since Nika was apparently on her way home from Oxford, that left the little family to converse among themselves about the erection of the shelter. They had made good progress that day. The foundation was dug and the curved metal shelter was put in place. Tomorrow they would need Rudi's help with the sandbags which had been delivered that afternoon.

When the family withdrew to listen to the BBC in the drawing room, Rudi could tell Hannah was about to excuse herself. He detained her by touching her briefly on the arm. "Could you spare me a minute or two? We can go into the library."

Her eyes were large in her face as though she were startled. She bit her lower lip. Finally, she said, "Of course, Rudi."

She preceded him into the book-lined room that smelled of pipe smoke and the roses his mother had arranged on the doctor's large walnut desk. There was a sofa under the window. They sat down next to one another. He had never known Hannah to be so spiritless, and it alarmed him.

"Was Samuel very hard on you yesterday?"

"He pointed out a few home truths," she said, her eyes on the clenched hands in her lap.

He rested his palm over them. "Hannah, please look at me."

She looked up and wetted her lips with her tongue. "I leave tomorrow," she said.

"I know. I am going to miss you terribly, but I will take happy memories of yesterday with me every time I go up in my Spitfire."

Clutching his hands, she said, "If you are in a southeast squadron, I will be able to track you from Uxbridge."

"I don't know if that's good or bad," Rudi replied. "You will worry every time I sortie."

"But I have to know. It would be far worse if I didn't know. If I was left guessing day after day . . . I think I would go mad."

"You care that much?"

Tears spilled over onto Hannah's cheeks. "For my sins."

Rudi pulled his gift out of his trouser pocket. "I care that much, as well." He put the small box in her hands. "I couldn't let you leave without giving you a remembrance."

She turned the box, inspecting it. "Not a ring!"

"No. I am not so presumptuous. A token only. Samuel never has to see it. It is between you and me. Like I said, a remembrance of all we have shared."

Hannah opened the package. When she saw the diamond lying on the black velvet, she drew a sharp breath. "Oh, Rudi. It is lovely. But it is too much. I shouldn't accept it."

Heart thundering, Rudi removed the pendant and chain from the box. "Let me fasten it for you. I want to see it on you."

Once he had it in place, Hannah threw her arms around his neck and resting her forehead on his shoulder she sobbed. "This is too hard. I never should have come to London. Now I can't let you go."

A wave of tenderness swept over him. He clasped her tightly in his arms. "We must be brave," he whispered into her hair. "You know how to do that, Hannah. You are one of the bravest people I know. You didn't turn a hair at Dunkirk."

"That shows what you know. When you were shot, I nearly fainted."

She finally let him go and looked into his eyes. "I am not a person given to prayer. But I will be praying for you."

"This is something I must do," Rudi said, trying to keep his emotions under control, trying not to let the least hint of fear or uncertainty into his voice. "I have known it ever since my father was killed on that mountain. The fight for Britain is vital. If we lose it, Hitler rules Europe. I must do my bit."

Letting him go, she took a handkerchief out of her pocket and tended to her tears. "I know that. I really do, Rudi. God be with you."

"I believe He will be. Now, do you report to Uxbridge in the afternoon?"

"Yes. I take the morning train to Dover. But I can't go through this again. Let us say our good-byes now. I will take a taxi to the station on my own."

"If that is what you want."

"It is. This war is bound to be full of good-byes. I surely hope I get better at them."

Every impulse he possessed urged Rudi to kiss her, but he held back. He didn't want her to have regrets she would have to make right with Samuel. Hannah had to see her way through her feelings alone.

"This is good-bye, then," he said.

"I will cherish my necklace. I shall wear it under my uniform. I wish I had something to give you."

"Your handkerchief will do," he said, smiling.

"But it is wet through!"

"I shall have it laundered and carry it with me each time I go up."

"Oh, Rudi . . ." She surrendered the scrap of cloth and lace. "You are wonderful beyond words. You must let me go now, before I break down again."

"All right," he said. As he let her go and watched her walk out of the library, Rudi was aware that the most important words remained unsaid between them.

{ 9 }

Anthony's days at the Foreign Office were long and grim throughout the month of June as France experienced the misery of defeat. Back in March, a joint resolve had been signed by Britain and France that neither country would surrender without the agreement of the other. Lord Halifax spent long hours with the War Cabinet and with his French counterparts, trying to rally the French government to remove itself to its African colonies and fight the war with the resources of its navy and empire from there. Defeatist elements, led by Marshal Pétain, wished to explore conditions of surrender without Britain's agreement. Churchill maintained that the two countries could still bring about the total defeat of Hitler if they worked together. Anthony's part in all this was to read incoming dispatches from foreign secretaries abroad and deal with them as best he might, leaving his chief, Lord Halifax, free to concentrate on France.

On 17 June, Anthony was dining at The Laurels, bound by protocol from discussing with his friends the struggles they were having with their now reluctant ally. That evening, the Prime Minister chose to address his people with a broadcast over the BBC. They sat in the white and gold drawing room, listening to his somber tones:

The news from France is very bad and I grieve for the gallant French people who have fallen into this terrible misfortune. Nothing will alter our feelings toward them or our faith that the genius of France will rise again. What has happened in France makes no difference to our actions and purpose. We have become the sole champions now in arms to defend the world cause. We shall do our best to be worthy of this high honor. We shall defend our island home, and with the British Empire we shall fight on unconquerable until the curse of Hitler is lifted from the brows of mankind. We are sure that in the end all will come right.

"Well, we can't say we didn't know that was coming," said Christian. "What of our soldiers in France?"

"They are on their way back here along with the Polish Free Army. General de Gaulle—the lone French general opposed to the surrender—also made it out by plane,"said Anthony.

Amalia said, "It is hard to believe that the French could fall so fast. I don't understand why they didn't retire the government to their African colonies and fight on. They have the largest army in Europe."

Anthony hesitated. Finally, he spoke. "I suppose I can tell you this much. My chief personally made every effort to spur the French government to fight on in the closest possible relationship with Her Majesty's Government, but the French declined. It is to Lord Halifax's chagrin that the defeatists are in power now, and his counterparts in France seemed to favor collaboration with Hitler rather than uniting their efforts with us. Of course, it would not do for the general public to know this. Hence Churchill's speech tonight."

"The French, they have made a terrible mistake," Nika said in her heavily accented English. "I thank the *bon Dieu* that my country's army comes here."

"Churchill will address Parliament tomorrow," Anthony said. "I imagine it will be a memorable speech. I must tell you we are devilishly lucky to have him at our helm. He will not let us go down the path that France has trodden. I don't know when the man sleeps. He goes forward on all fronts at once. During this whole French tragedy I know he has kept in close contact with President Roosevelt. He has supervised the huge project of Home Defense measures, has organized the forces in the Dominions, and supervised the production of armaments and tanks."

"If we had had a man of his stature and convictions in Austria, it would have made all the difference," said Amalia.

"He is a peculiarly British phenomenon, I am afraid, darling," said Zaleski.

When Nika walked Anthony to the door, he managed a short conversation with her. "Have you heard anything from Irene about a post at Somerville?" he asked.

"Yes. She is very kind. And you were right. Oxford is enchanting. The college will make me an offer soon for the term next autumn. I have decided to volunteer as a nurse's aide in the meantime. Amalia is taking me to the hospital tomorrow to begin my training."

"Jolly good. You will do splendidly. You have been on my mind. I hope you know that I would like to have been around more, but the government is rather in crisis at the moment."

She gave a mirthless laugh. "I defer gladly to affairs of state under the circumstances. I would be surprised to hear that you get any sleep."

"I manage. I'm afraid I must wish you cheerio now. Good luck with your training." Impulsively, he leaned down and kissed her on the cheek.

"Good night, Anthony," she said, her voice soft.

On the morning of the nineteenth, Anthony read the text of Churchill's speech to Parliament from the previous evening. It was much as he had predicted.

What [French] General Weygand called the Battle of France is over. I expect that the Battle of Britain is about to begin. Upon this battle depends the survival of Christian civilization . . . The whole fury and might of the enemy must very shortly be turned upon us. Hitler knows that he will have to break us in this island or lose the war. If we can stand up to him, all Europe may be free and the life of the world may move forward into broad sunlit uplands. Let us therefore brace ourselves to our duties, and so bear ourselves that, if the British Empire and its Commonwealth last for a thousand years, men will say "This was their finest hour."

Anthony could not help being braced up by the words. He wondered if Amalia had translated them for Nika. Ringing Laurel House, he asked to speak with her.

She greeted him in French. "If your Prime Minister could win this war with rhetoric, I would feel very reassured indeed."

"He is a gifted speaker, Nika, but I believe he truly reflects the mood of the land. Did you sign up for your training?"

"Yes. As a matter of fact, I must be off. I'm due at the hospital shortly."

"Good luck. Remember I'm thinking of you."

His friend Reston, who he had imagined to be, like him, occupied with the press of work, strolled into his office. He indicated the newspaper. "The man's a wonder, isn't he?"

"I hate to think of what it would be to face this crisis with Chamberlain still at the helm. I have a feeling we'd be going to Hitler, hat in hand," Anthony stated.

"What have you been up to?"

"Mainly keeping the chief apprised of the Italian situation, among other things. I never realized Halifax felt so strongly about France. This defeat has knocked the wind out of him."

"I agree. That proposition of a union with France took even Churchill by surprise. I'm told that he didn't like it at all, at first."

"Yes, I'd heard that," said Anthony. "And for all Halifax's generous impulses, I'm told the French took it as an insult! They'd rather be a vassal state to Germany than what they understood to be a dominion of the British Empire."

Reston gave a brief half-smile. "I guess no matter how dire their straits, the French will still be the French. Now the matter that presses is their fleet."

"I have a hard time believing Hitler will allow those prize French ships to sail away into our care and keeping," Anthony said with a sense of dread.

"What do you think Churchill will do? He is a navy man, after all."

"If they won't consent to join in our fight, or at least sail to the West Indies, I hope he blows them up."

"And world opinion? That matters nothing to you?"

"We have to take care of ourselves if no one else is going help us."

Reston harrumphed. "Fotheringill, I feel I must remind you that Churchill is not God. There is danger in putting all our confidence in him. The country seems to believe that the man is omniscient and cannot err. Just because he says something doesn't make it so, old man."

Anger shot through Anthony at the words. "He is doing his best to hold the country together and press forward with hope. Hope is a commodity that can make all the difference, Reston. Without it, we are finished. If you are going to talk like a defeatist, I would ask you to stay out of my office."

Reston's eyebrows rose at this outburst. "I'm not a defeatist, but I am a realist," he said as he left the office.

Anthony tried to shake off the encounter. He was disappointed in Reston. They had been at Oxford together after the late war and had remained close. Since Reston was a widower with no intention of remarrying, he had kept Anthony company during all these years of Madge's desertion. Both opera fans, they had enjoyed many a season together, as well as the occasional night at the theater. Nigel Reston had the kind of good looks that attracted women. Suave, with thick, smooth brown hair, bright blue eyes, and regular features, he dressed with flair. There had been women in his life over the years, but no one permanent. They seldom discussed work, but Anthony had been aware that the man had stood in the appeasement camp. Surely he must see what a mistake that had been?

He had the sense now that something deeper lay on the man's mind. He was definitely soured. Anthony shouldn't have had to warn him about defeatist talk.

With an effort, he settled down to concentrate on his effort to draft an invitation to August Zaleski, Andrzej's cousin and the Foreign Secretary of the Polish Government-in-Exile. He proposed, on behalf of Lord Halifax, that the two men meet to discuss the terms of their government and military collaboration through the coming months.

Eventually, this brought Anthony around to thoughts of Nika. Though she was a desirable woman, his interest in her went deeper than the physical. He thought about her endurance through the siege of Warsaw and the pluck she had shown to escape Poland on her own. Despite her sadness and fear, he could detect steel in her, though she seemed to discount it. He couldn't help but compare her to his ex-wife, who had never been able to adjust to the realities of the first war, even after it had ended.

With sudden resolution, he rang a florist he found in the telephone directory and ordered a bouquet of spring flowers to be delivered to Nika at Laurel House. "Hope your day went well," were the words he dictated for the card.

Christian knew he was a very young recruit for MI5, but the recommendation that he be hired had come from the Prime Minister himself. He and Mr. Churchill had worked together before the war when he was only sixteen. The work he had now was similar to what he had done then: to infiltrate fifth columnists who were preparing for Britain to become a Nazi state after a hoped-for invasion.

With a new name—Neuburg—and a new personal history, he was settled back at Oxford in a new college—Christ Church— where it was hoped he would attract recruiters to the Nazi cause. All his old friends from Balliol had joined up either in the

Army or the RAF. Most of the males left at Oxford were for-
eigners, many of them Americans.

Christian had always loved sailing close to the wind. Today
he made his way to a student pub, the Boar's Head, that Rudi
had told him about. It was located above a green grocer on the
High. Under his scholar's black robe, he wore expensive tweed
slacks and a matching jacket, his blond hair fashionably styled
straight back from his forehead.

His brother had met Germans of all stations in this pub before the war. Christian expected that most of them had left and
joined the German army. Now the pub, with its nickel-plated
bar and window shades darkening the daylight, contained only a
few students who were drinking and playing darts or chess.

Ordering a pint of bitters, he found a stool at the bar that en-
abled him to watch the dart game. The players were Americans.

"Did your old man send you the money?" a stocky redhead
asked his gangly, blond opponent.

"Not yet. I can't figure what's holding him up."

"Hey! Good throw. Do you need a loan?"

"Naw, I can manage," the skinny blond said, hitting the bull's
eye again. He turned to Chris. "D'you play darts?"

Christian stood and held out his hand. Having spent months
studying American films and being excellent with languages
and dialects, he said his name with an American inflection,
"Neuburg. Yeah, I love a good game of darts."

"Heinemann," the rangy blond said, shaking his hand. "This
is Fromm."

The redhead shook hands. His red cheeks gave him a cheru-
bic look. "Where're you from?"

"Chicago," said Chris.

"No kiddin'?" said Fromm. "I'm from Milwaukee."

Chris's American geography was not great, so he could only assume the cities were close to one another. "Small world."

"Detroit," said Heinemann. Chris knew enough to know that Detroit was the automobile capital of the US.

"Let's have a game then," said Chris.

Chris let each of the Americans win, then won the third and fourth games, earning him a free pint as they sat at a table beside the shaded window. The Americans pulled out cigarettes.

"So what are you studying?" Heinemann asked Chris, tapping his unlit cigarette on the expensive face of his gold wristwatch. His clothes under his black scholar's robe were of costly tweed. Chris could tell that the lapels of his jacket were hand stitched.

"Greats," Chris said, glad that at least this much was true. "You?"

"I'm doing Philosophy. Fromm is Modern Politics. Where do you live in Chicago?"

"North Shore," Chris named the area his studies had told him was the most exclusive and wealthy area. "Evanston."

"Evanston is great," said Fromm said. "Milwaukee is boring." His jacket, though obviously expensive was a loud check over a plaid shirt.

"So is Detroit," said Heinemann, running a hand through his thick blond mane, making it stand on end. "Everyone in my suburb is in management for one of the car companies."

"What d'you guys think of Oxford?" Chris asked.

Fromm shrugged. "It's the same here, really. Upper class. I don't know when the last time was that anyone had a new idea."

Instinct made Chris play to this discontent. "I hear you. It's a lot like the North Shore."

"Think you'll stick it out?" asked Heinemann.

"Yeah," said Chris. "It's a new experience culturally. I like my studies, even if the Brits are a bit stodgy."

Fromm said, "Anthropologically speaking, this whole war set-up is interesting. Something about war seems to bring out the root tendencies of each nation."

Chris asked, "What do you see as the root characteristic of the British?"

"Insularity, definitely. They've never really been a part of Europe," the redheaded Fromm said, flicking his cigarette ash on the floor. "They think they're superior."

Heinemann added, "They're a bunch of pit bulls. But I wonder how long they'll last when the bombing starts?"

"How would you characterize the Germans?" asked Chris.

Heinemann drew on his cigarette. "Belligerent, certainly. Mystical."

"Mystical?" echoed Chris.

Fromm leaned forward on his elbows. "This whole Nazi drivel is based on the Wagner mystic. Nordic tradition."

"It may be drivel," Chris argued, "but it's powerful drivel. I don't think an army that can fight the way they do is driven by some opera composer."

"Of course not," Heinemann said airily. "They're driven by the knowledge that they're a race apart, that they deserve to rule Europe. Hitler's ideals. But those same ideals are steeped in mysticism."

"Interesting viewpoint," said Chris, simulating thoughtfulness. Heinemann had slipped there, shown a little too much admiration. "I'm hungry. Do they have anything decent to eat in this place?"

"Meat pies," Heinemann said.

They each ordered a couple of meat pies, and the discussion became more general. Chris learned that they spent most evenings in the pub. Since this was their third year at Oxford, and until the outbreak of the war this had been a German student favorite, he figured they had known many Germans, and most probably some of Nazi persuasion.

Leaving that evening, he thought that thanks to Rudi's tip about the pub, he hadn't done badly for his first day on the job.

{ 10 }

"If you were a baroness before you married Andrzej, how did you ever become a nurse?" Nika asked Amalia as they drank tea in the deserted hospital cafeteria during their delayed break. Her first day as a nurse's aide was going well, largely because she had been assigned to train under her friend, who made even her gray and white chambray uniform look elegant.

"It is a long story," Amalia said with a slow smile. "I was married to a German officer in the first war. I had very conflicted feelings about that war. To make things more miserable, I was living with my mother-in-law in Berlin. I needed to do something with myself—I was going mad.

"So I signed up to be a nurse's aide, as you have done. When my husband was killed, I went home to Vienna. They were so short on qualified nurses, they allowed aides to qualify by taking an exam, which I did." Her friend had a faraway look, lost in her memories.

"Andrzej says you worked together at University Hospital."

"Yes. Until he left to fight on the front on the side of the English and French. There was a horrible misunderstanding between us after the war and I married an Austrian baron. My nursing days came to an end."

"My heavens," said Nika. "What a story! How long were you married to the baron?" The more Nika learned about Amalia, the more intrigued she became.

"Twenty years. He was my sons' father. A very good man. Rudi takes after him."

"And he was killed by the Nazis?"

"As we were trying to escape after the *Anschluss*." Amalia shivered. "Andrzej was there. He was helping us."

Nika longed to know more, but she restrained her curiosity. "I can tell this is a very long and complicated business. Thank you for sharing it with me."

As sometimes happened since coming to England, she felt an acute sense of loneliness. The color went out of the day and she slumped a bit in her chair.

"I can't even imagine what it must have been like for you to be in that horrific siege . . . to have the bombing every day and to see your parents die in front of you," Amalia said. "You must have nightmares."

Was Amalia a mind-reader? "It is worse than nightmares," Nika said. "Everything comes back to me when I am trying to sleep. I see everything, feel everything, just like I did when I was going through it. I actually get very little sleep."

Amalia's brow puckered and her eyes took on a sadness Nika hadn't seen there before. "In the last war, we called that shell shock. My first husband suffered from it. It was brutal." Amalia took a deep breath. "I failed him. What can I do to help you, Ni-ka?"

She had never thought of asking anyone for help. The offer surprised her and filled the loneliness for a moment. "You are so kind," Nika said. "Perhaps you can tell me how you got through the awful times?"

"I don't know that I am one to give advice. I would have died when Eberhard died, if it weren't for my friend Louisa. She convinced me to hold on. Just to take things one day at a time. She told me that eventually I would see the light again." Amalia reached for Nika's hand across the table. "She was right. I know you are worried about what is coming to us here. But we are your family now. We will stand by you." Amalia smiled wholeheartedly. "Andrzej has loved you and your family for years. And I suspect Anthony has a strong attachment to you as well." She squeezed Nika's hand. "Louisa stood by me. That made all the difference. With her love and devotion she convinced me there was a God. He and we won't leave you, Nika. Together, we will stand firm."

Tears poured down Nika's cheeks as Amalia spoke, and she began shaking with sobs. Amalia knelt by her side, and taking her in her arms, let her cry. It felt so good to have another human being hold her. Warmth flowed into the frozen wasteland within her.

"You are so good to me," she finally said as her sobs waned. "I am not nearly as strong as you are."

"I don't believe that," her friend said. "You could have given into grief and remained in Warsaw to be killed yourself. But somehow you mustered the strength to leave."

"I should have stayed and buried my parents. I am haunted by their broken bodies lying in that basement."

"Nika, don't you realize that their dearest wish would have been for you to escape, to live?"

Wiping her face with her handkerchief, she felt a kind of absolution at Amalia's words. They were true, of course. Guilt she didn't even realize she carried was assuaged.

"Thank you," she whispered, her voice hoarse. "You have helped me more than you could possibly realize."

"I am glad. I only hope that when things get to be too much that you will come to me and talk it through. Love heals. I think it is the only thing that does."

Nika nodded, unable to form words at this generosity. She allowed herself to feel the stirrings of hope.

Amalia continued, "Let's just take things one day at a time. You are going to make an excellent aide. You have the compassion required and you are a hard worker. Fortunately, nowadays they have other people to scrub the floors."

"You had to scrub floors?"

"For my sins."

They finished their tea, and returned to their unit on the third floor. Amalia made her rounds, checking bandages, and changing them where necessary. Nika watched carefully, as this would be one of her duties. She knew the time would come when this comparatively empty ward would be packed with wounded. The sooner she learned her duties the better.

Watching Amalia change a the bandage of a RAF pilot whose arm had been amputated, she thought of Anthony's story and her heart was sore. Her indignation against Madge grew. How could the woman have left the dear man when he was suffering so? He would have felt tremendous physical pain, and then the rejection of the woman he loved. And she had taken his daughter away as well. Nika could not imagine how he must have suffered. No wonder he had never married again.

Nika followed Amalia to the next bed where she checked the morphine IV for a pilot who was suffering from a shattered shoulder joint. Next there was a head wound.

These RAF men were unmistakably British, she realized. None of them complained. They chatted to one another as though they were experiencing nothing but a slight inconvenience. From what she could gather, they all expressed concern about whether they would be able to fly again.

The last thing in the afternoon was for Amalia to dispense medications. Since that would always be the job of a registered nurse and not an aide, Nika was left to inventory the existing medicines in the cupboard and note their numbers carefully in the log with the exact time.

At five o'clock, they joined the other hospital employees on the Underground home. After Nika had changed her uniform, she met Amalia for tea in the upstairs yellow sitting room. With its floral chintz upholstery and matching drapes, it reminded Nika of an Impressionist painting.

"Andrzej rang to say he must work a double shift. He won't be home until midnight," her hostess told her.

"Poor Andrzej," said Nika. "He will be out on his feet. Have you heard from Rudi lately?"

"Since France has fallen, they're all on high alert, expecting air attacks to begin at any time over the Channel. The fellows we saw in the hospital today sustained their injuries while they were providing air cover during the Dunkirk evacuation. They are the tip of the iceberg, I fear."

At that moment, Sims entered the room carrying an enormous bouquet of spring flowers. To Nika's surprise, he carried it to her.

It could only be from Anthony. She read his card and found herself blushing. Thanking Sims, she walked over and set the vase on the mantle.

"How very kind," she said to Amalia. "They're from Anthony, with hopes that my day went well."

"Time for a change of subject." After Amalia poured out their tea and passed jam sandwiches, she said, "Are you and dear Anthony in the process of becoming an item?"

Nika took a sip of tea, but it was still hot and she burned her tongue. "I don't know. He has certainly been very kind to me."

"He was dreadfully hurt by Madge, you know."

Nika grew angry again at the thought of what he had endured. "I don't understand that woman! She is without a heart, I am certain."

"I was shocked when he told me the story, as well."

"Does he ever see his daughter?"

"Not much. At any rate, they are not close."

"She must be heartless also. Anthony is one of the loveliest men I have ever met."

"I agree. He opened his home to us when we came here from Austria. He and Andrzej are great friends."

Suddenly restless, Nika set down her teacup and began pacing the room, changing the subject to their plans to finish off the inside of the Anderson shelter. After tea, she went up to her white bedroom with the forget-me-not blue duvet and slipper chair. Taking all the pins from her hair, she shook it out and brushed it. More comfortable, she lay down on her bed and closed her eyes, intending to nap before dinner.

Sleep would not come, however. Instead, she thought of Anthony, wondering if she could ever trust her heart again. The wounds her marriage had wrought were ever with her.

Nika was wrestling to compose a paper on the concept of death in Anna Karenina *when her father was shown into her study one evening.*

"Papa! How good to see you!"

As his powerful arms embraced her, she felt that he clung a little too tightly, that he was afraid to let her go.

"Nika, dear, I have come to speak to you about a serious matter. Perhaps you are already aware, but if you are not, you should be."

Her heart took a dive. She knew this could only be about Bazyli whom her father had never liked. Feeling a sudden chill, she seated herself next to the fireplace. "What is it, Papa?"

"Your husband is keeping an opera dancer. He is faithless. And as he is also without a fortune of his own, it is your money which is paying her bills."

Bazyli. Unfaithful. It could not be. "Papa, you must be mistaken. He loves me. I am certain he does. We are going to have a child."

"Men like Bazyli can love their wives and still keep mistresses. It is a fact of life in his circle. He may even have more than one."

Everything in her fought against this revelation. She lashed out at her father, "How can you wound me so? You are glad, aren't you? You never wanted me to marry him."

"His personality is larger than life, Nika. I knew that one woman would never be enough for someone like him."

These words had the ring of truth. Bazyli was a man who loved and embraced everyone he met. With her, he made love with an intensity that carried her away. And it seemed he was never satisfied. With his extreme good looks, it did not surprise her that other women were attracted to him. But they were expecting a child!

Pain lanced her beneath her breastbone and shredded her heart. Baz with another woman. The searing pain made it hard for her to breathe. Then she remembered the other part of her father's message: she was paying to support the woman!

"Where is she?" Nika demanded. "Where does she live?"

Her father's face flushed with alarm. "I cannot tell you that! It is not fit that you should meet such a person! Do not even think of lowering yourself in such a way."

She would not let this pain get the best of her. When Bazyli returned tonight, she would confront him. If he did not get rid of this mistress, she would tell him to leave her! She would make him choose between them.

A storm of tears overtook her and she collapsed on the couch.

Papa said, "I will call your mother. You are going to make yourself ill, Nika. He is not worth it. Think of the baby."

Later that night, the police had come to tell her of Bazyli's death in the motor crash. As Nika fought her grief in the turbulent weeks that followed, she had suffered a miscarriage. Those memories were blacked out, beyond her reach. She dared not go there. It had taken over a year for her to climb out of that abyss.

She had barred her heart against anyone else in the ten years since, concentrating on her career in academia, which was an excellent place to hide. Now she was starting over: she had no family, no home, no academic position. She was exposed and raw from the loss of everything, one small being tossed in a maelstrom of tragedy that was sweeping away the world she had known.

How was she to embark on a relationship that would require her to put all her tragedies aside and have hope for the future? Was she just drawn to Anthony because she was trying to ground herself? To find a place to land? Surely it was the worst of all times to begin a love affair.

Hannah found her work in the WAAFs fascinating. As she trained for her job in an underground bunker fifty feet below ground, she learned many new skills.

First, she learned to read the device that was called radar, short for Radio Detection and Ranging. Towers built along the coast sent out radio waves which would detect incoming planes from France and pinpoint their location. For now they were practicing by reading the RAF planes that patrolled the Navy convoys in the Channel, but any day now they expected the *Luftwaffe* to be attacking from bases in France. When that happened, Hannah and her fellow radar readers would report the attackers' positions by radio transmission to the RAF squadrons, who would then scramble for their Spitfires or Hurricane fighter planes, take off, and give battle to the *Luftwaffe's Messerschmitt* fighters at their known location. WAAF plotters would push blocks across a map of the Channel, keeping track of enemy and RAF engagements in the air.

Radar was a closely kept secret, and Hannah realized that though the RAF was outnumbered by the *Luftwaffe*, it gave them an advantage—the edge they needed to win the upcoming battle for Britain. She was very glad she had managed to get such a helpful post in that fight.

She had two bunkmates in a Quonset hut not far from the dugout where she worked. In that quaint tradition so notably British, they all referred to one another by their last names.

"Gluck, have you any talcum powder?" Sandra Tanner asked her. "Somehow I let myself run out and the store's still shut up."

"I'll trade for some tooth powder," Hannah replied. "Why *is* the store shut up?"

"That, my girl, is known only to the powers that be," responded Nellie Josephs. "I'm off for my bit of breakfast. Anyone joining me?"

"I'm coming," said Hannah, pulling on her uniform jacket and hat. Though it was late June, mornings were definitely chilly along the coast.

Josephs was a brisk walker. "D'you think Jerry will attack today?" she asked.

"My bet is that they're still getting things mopped up in France and repositioning themselves, but you never know," said Hannah. "One thing about the Germans is their incredible hunger for new territory. And we all know we're next on the menu."

Silence greeted her reply. Then, "My chap is in the RAF. I'm all nerves."

"Radar gives us the advantage," said Hannah. "Those *Messerschmitt*'s are going to figure we are magicians, always turning up right where they are."

They had reached the canteen. Hannah had to force herself to eat. In the morning, all she could manage was a boiled egg and coffee. She thought about the coming battle morning, noon, and night. Rudi's determined face was always before her.

As she sliced the top off her egg, her bunkmate said, "Are you going to tell me about that great rock you're wearing around your neck?"

Hannah started, feeling at her neckline. Somehow, Rudi's diamond had slipped to the outside of her collar. "It's a memento from my closest friend."

"Friend? Not your fiancé?"

"Right."

"Hmm. Every girl should have a friend like that."

Hannah felt the familiar churn of guilt in her stomach. She didn't reply. She had had one letter from Rudi, but he couldn't tell her where he was stationed. She felt it was somewhere along the coast, however, because he had talked about the weather over the Channel and how unpredictable it was.

She wished she could somehow sneak into his Spitfire, as she had accompanied him on the boat to Dunkirk. She didn't like being away from him when things were so dicey.

On the other hand, Samuel was not at all happy with her proximity to the airfields. He was certain she was going to be injured in an air raid. His lack of confidence annoyed her greatly.

{ 11 }

Rudi was so tired of hanging about the airfield that he was happy to volunteer for a reconnaissance mission. He was more than anxious try to find the airfields and the *Messerschmitts* lining up on the French coast. Goering's pride and joy. Well, they were ready for them!

He was instructed to fly high and to watch his fuel gauge. Climbing into his plane, which he'd named "Doom," he patted the side affectionately. Once inside, he pulled his canvas helmet and oxygen mask over his head. As he coasted down the short runway, he anticipated the familiar thrill of lift off. It was exhilarating every time. Soon he was over the green fields of his adopted country, and then in a moment over the Channel. He concentrated on flying in a straight line—the shortest distance between England and France. Once he had reached the coast of France, he climbed higher and turned slightly north.

It wasn't long before he located an area of heavy construction that he presumed to be a new airfield. Guarding it on both sides were *Messerschmitts* presumably ready to give a fight to anyone from above who threatened the new installation. Not anxious to be a target, he moved further north. By the time he headed for his base, he had located six parcels of French farmland that were being converted to bases—all with standby aircraft posting guard.

No sense sending bombers at this point. They would only be shot down by the fast climbing, heavily armed MEs. As it was, he was weaving in and out of anti-aircraft fire.

It was going to be an unrelenting fight. He well knew that the British had lost 500 planes and pilots in France. Thank heavens Churchill had held back the rest, though it had been against French wishes.

Flying back to Biggin Hill airfield before he spent any more fuel, Rudi set his jaw. He wished the battle would begin. He was anxious to take down a good many MEs and watch them tumble into the Channel below him.

Amalia received an unexpected guest one Saturday morning at the end of June. She and Nika had the day off and were busy knitting gray wool scarves for Rudi to wear when flying. Into the yellow parlor, Simms ushered Miss Sonia Fotheringill whom Amalia had not seen since she had completed her English tutoring the year before.

"Hello, Mrs. Zaleski," Sonia said in her quiet, almost shy way.

"Why, Sonia! How nice to see you," said Amalia, rising to greet her with a kiss on each cheek.

Nika took in the girl's appearance. She was very fair and apparently used no makeup, giving her face a rather blank expression, as though she were missing lashes and brows. Her clothing did nothing to help the impression she made—a celery-colored skirt with a celery and white striped blouse. Her blonde hair was rolled neatly around the back of her neck, held in place by a hair net. In stature, she was quite tall, almost as tall as Amalia.

"I thought I would just pop round and see how you are getting on," the young woman said. Her eyes kept straying to Nika.

"It's very nice to have you. Sonia, this is our friend, Nika. We will speak in French, if you don't mind. She has come to us from Poland by way of France. She was very close to my husband's family." Turning to Nika, Amalia said, "Sonia Fotheringill is my former English tutor and also Anthony's daughter."

Nika rose and shook the hand of the young woman. "Lovely to meet you, Miss Fotheringill."

They all sat down. "Call me Sonia, please. I saw my father in the Strand this morning. We had a quick cup of coffee. He told me about you." She smiled at Nika. "I owe him quite a large favor, as he recently bought me an automobile. He asked that I repay him by tutoring you in English."

"Oh, my heavens," said Nika struck by Anthony's thoughtfulness. "How extraordinarily kind. That would actually be very useful, as I am now working in an English hospital. I know very little of the language."

"I would be happy to teach you. I understand that my father thinks very highly of you. I was so sorry to hear of the death of your family."

Nika looked down in confusion at her words. This was all so unexpected. What else had Anthony told his daughter?

"Thank you for your concern. Most days, I feel very lucky to have escaped with my own life."

"My father thinks you are very brave." She turned to Amalia. "How are your sons, Mrs. Zaleski?"

"Busy. They have enlisted, of course. Rudi seems to have suddenly caught on to English all at once after his year and a half of lessons. I think one day he just faced it and wrestled it to the ground. I must confess, I never thought it would happen."

"And Christian is such a whiz!" Sonia said.

"They are very different," Amalia said. "What have you been doing with yourself lately?"

Nika sat back, content to listen to the conversation.

"I have been very busy. There are more Polish and Belgians arriving here all the time. Through my father, I have been put in touch with many of the more important ones who are forming governments here and want to learn English. I'm holding group classes for them."

"Excellent!" Amalia said.

Nika broke in, "You will not have time to teach me on my own. I can join one of the groups."

"My father was most particular. Besides, the groups are almost exclusively male. I think you will be more comfortable if I teach you in the evenings, when you come home from the hospital. When would be a good time?"

"We dine at eight o'clock," said Nika. "But we return from the hospital at four o'clock for tea. Perhaps after tea would be good?"

"Join us for tea," invited Amalia.

"That would be lovely," said Sonia. "Would Monday, Wednesday, and Friday work out for you?" she asked.

Nika began to notice that the young woman had a delicate charm of her own. It flashed out now and again with her smile. "Perfectly," said Nika. "Now, tell me," she couldn't resist asking, "how is your father? He must be working very hard just now with the fall of France."

"Yes. He can't speak of his work, but he looks harried." She smiled fondly. "He gets this funny little piece of his hair that sticks up in his crown when he is concerned and working too hard."

Nika softened at these words, trying to picture Anthony as less than perfectly dapper.

Sonia continued. "I have decided to move into that big monstrosity of a townhouse he lives in for the duration of the war. He definitely needs someone besides servants looking after him. Mama now has a husband to see to her whims."

Amalia said, "I am sure that would mean a great deal to him, Sonia. He is very fond of you, you know."

The woman smiled one of her sweet smiles and stood up. "Very well. Shall we begin Monday, then?"

"That would suit me splendidly. Do I need to purchase a grammar or something?" Nika asked.

"I have everything you need. You can reimburse me, if you like."

"Splendid. I appreciate this so much, Sonia."

After the girl had left, Amalia raised an eyebrow. "Mr. Fotheringill is certainly watching after your interests."

Nika gave a little laugh and said, "I am so glad she is moving in with her father. That will mean a great deal to him, you know."

"Yes. Although he has seen little of her during her life, I know he is very fond and proud of her."

"She seems very sweet. I hope I shall take to English. I am most anxious to be able to communicate."

"You obviously have skill with languages, Nika. Rudi and I were probably her most difficult pupils!"

$\mathcal{D}$

Christian continued to visit the Boar's Head, where he had met the two Americans, Heinemann and Fromm. He had studied maps and travel books about Detroit and Milwaukee and come to the conclusion that he wouldn't like to live in either place. Contacts at MI5 had been useful in determining the German populations of both cities were large. There were a significant number of pro-Nazi organizations in both places.

Meanwhile, Chris determined that both students were of above average intelligence and means. Heinemann had better taste than Fromm and was very likely of a higher social standing. Both were much better at chess than they were at darts.

As he was playing a game of chess with Fromm one afternoon, he let fall a chagrined, "*Ach, du lieber . . . ,*" when his partner called checkmate.

"You still speak German at home, eh Neuburg?"

Chris simulated embarrassment and ran a hand through his hair. "Sometimes."

"You had better watch that around here. You never know who might take it the wrong way. Did your parents immigrate to the US recently?"

"My grandparents did. My grandfather still lives with us," Chris told him.

Fromm raised an eyebrow. "Politics?"

Chris had given this matter considerable thought and study. Now he was able to say, "Grandfather is a Prussian. I was raised on those old Nordic legends you were talking about."

Heinemann had been listening to the conversation from the next table. Now he leaned over and said in a low voice, "*Sprechen sie Deutsch?*"

In his best Prussian accent, Chris replied that of course he spoke German. Keeping his voice down, he also said that while British beer was all right, he missed the German lager he had at home in Chicago brewed by the Germans on the West Side.

The men exchanged a look. "Why did you come to Oxford?" Heinemann asked.

Chris manufactured a sigh. "My mother is British. First generation in America. She doesn't think any college in the US is good enough for her Golden Boy. And I must admit, it is a great learning environment. I am really enjoying myself. I think it would be more fun, however, if there were more Englishmen our age around, but of course they are all off preparing to fight." He removed his pieces from the chess board, stacking them up on his side of the table. "Either of you want another game?"

He longed to asked them what they thought of the war, but he judged it to be too soon for confidences about that. Trying very hard to keep in tune with the little guiding voice inside him, Christian was confident that when the time was right, they would talk to him.

Anthony was always to remember those crowded days of June, 1940, as possessing the same frantic, cramming atmosphere as he felt during his Oxford years the week before exams. There was such a crush of things to think about, to get in order before the ultimate defense of their Island began. Very uppermost in Churchill's mind was the French fleet. The Foreign Office had tentative relations with the new Vichy collaborative government, but this did not amount to anything of significance. In the end, Admiral Darlan, commander of the fleet, took up Vichy's offer as the equivalent of First Lord of the Admiralty of Vichy France, choosing this position over promises made to Britain that he would never allow the French fleet to fall into German hands.

The decision to blow up the French fleet and cause a complete schism with their one time ally was not taken lightly, but it was taken. As a Foreign Office Undersecretary, Anthony understood that when this Operation Catapult was carried out on July 3, the probable reaction of foreign interests was weighed carefully in the balance.

His office was invited—indeed required—to attend the speech given by the Prime Minister in Parliament on this occasion. After stating that they were on the "eve of an attempted invasion" and expected to "maintain a spirit of alert and confident energy," he gave solemn warnings that went straight to Anthony's heart. He hoped that his friend Reston was listening.

The Prime Minister expects all His Majesty's servants in high places to set an example of steadiness and resolution. They should check and rebuke the expression of loose and ill–digested opinions in their circles, or by their subordinates. They should not hesitate to report, or if necessary remove, any person, officers, or officials who are found to be consciously exercising a disturbing or depressing influence, and whose talk is calculated to spread alarm and despondency.

After the speech which received loud ovations from the House, Anthony took a cab to The Laurels to share the PM's message with Zaleski. The two men sat in his library, smoking their pipes.

"What has been foreign reaction to the bombing?" Zaleski asked.

"I didn't properly appreciate it at the time the decision was made, but it was the first belligerent act we've taken defining our actual intention of fighting on alone. With the exception of France and Germany, the reaction has been positive. We have stepped over the line and committed ourselves."

"I say, 'Bravo, Churchill.' Let's get this battle underway," said Zaleski.

"It's surprising how public opinion has turned. That is exactly how the man in the street seems to feel. 'Bring it on. We're ready.'"

{ 12 }

Air Chief Marshal Hugh Dowding strode before Rudi's squadron as they stood at attention on Biggin Hill Airfield early in the morning of July 10th.

"We have a convoy of ships passing through the Channel today, so this may very well be our first day of this new battle. Remember, you have only fifteen seconds of ammunition. You know what the drill is. You come in high, flying out of the sun. You shoot the *Messerschmitts* out of the sky. We are heavily outnumbered, so you must make every advantage count. They will not be expecting you to appear so quickly at their coordinates.

"Goering is overconfident because of the great number of aircraft he has. You won't get lost up there if you follow Fighter Command on your headsets. They won't let you down.

"Jerry will send in the Stuka bombers escorted by the MEs. Shoot down the MEs first before they can get you. Then go for the bombers. Questions?"

No one in Rudi's squadron was fool enough to ask questions. They had drilled for this exact scenario too many times. Today, it looked like they were finally going to engage the enemy in the fight for Britain. He knew it was dangerous, but he was ready. He had even put Hannah's handkerchief in his pocket. His Spitfire was in tip-top shape. They were only waiting the signal to scramble for their planes.

At 13:35 hours the signal came. Rudi shrugged into his leather jacket and gloves as he ran for his plane. Once he had leapt into his Spitfire he donned his leather helmet, oxygen mask, and head phones. He pressed the starter and rolled his plane out to take off from the airfield in formation.

As he ascended into the sky, his heart lifted and Rudi felt that he was doing what he had been born to do. The weather was clear today—the sky bright blue clear down to the Channel below him. Soon he was able to see the convoy of ships. Through his headphones, the coordinates of the enemy aircraft were repeated. Though he kept his eyes ahead, looking to spy his target, and was careful to remain in formation, he sensed the presence of many planes in the air with him.

And suddenly they were there, the *Luftwaffe's Messerschmitts* dead ahead with their black crosses. Rudi banked his Spitfire and climbed above them. As soon as he had one in range, he let go a burst of ammunition. Missing, he cursed himself. Beginner's nerves! He didn't miss the next one. Or the next. With great satisfaction, he saw them spiral into the Channel below. As an ME came straight for him, he banked again and climbed above it, shooting straight into the cockpit, but he was out of ammunition. He headed back to Biggin Hill, his heart singing. Taking Hannah's handkerchief from his pocket, he kissed it. "We did it!"

When he got to the airfield, he refueled and loaded more ammunition. As soon as two more Spitfires were ready, they took off in formation. This sortie was not as successful for Rudi. As he was swooping in to fire, an ME had him in its sights and a burst of ammunition set one of his wings on fire. Banking swiftly, he took himself out of range and, praying all the way, he headed for land. As soon as he was across the white cliffs, he landed roughly in a field, radioing for help as he went down. Rudi told himself he had been an overconfident idiot. The incident could have been much worse.

At Uxbridge, fifty feet below ground Hannah was sitting in the Operations Room at the radar screen when she spied the first MEs flying in formation out over the channel. Reading their coordinates, she radioed the message to fighter command. From there she knew it would be sent to the fighter squadrons and the women who plotted the conflict over the Channel on the huge map that she could see over the railing in the room below her. Her insides turned to water as she sighted more and more aircraft leaving the French shores. The RAF was certainly going to be outnumbered.

Hannah kept her voice level and continued to report enemy positions and trajectory.

Soon she saw the RAF meet the enemy and several aircraft spiraled off radar, disappearing off the screen. As they mixed it up, she was unable to tell which were the enemy and which were

RAF. Her gut clenched and she wondered if any of those lost were Rudi. She could scarcely focus.

Then, almost as quickly as it had begun, it was over. Planes began returning to base. Hannah sat staring at the empty screen. So fast! The battle itself had only lasted twenty minutes.

Everything remained quiet around her in the bunker. She stayed at her post, her burning eyes still focused on the screen. How soon would she even know if Rudi had been in one of those planes that had gone down? She had thought she would gain that information serving in this position, but she didn't.

Hannah chastised herself. She couldn't live like this day after day. She was going to have to find a way to cope. Otherwise, she wasn't going to be able to do her job.

She looked over the rail at the plotters. They had resumed their seats, picking up books, reading as though nothing had happened. The phlegmatic English! Hannah was a passionate Viennese. The man she loved might just have been killed, sent spiraling to his death in the Channel.

There, I finally acknowledged it. Rudi, not Samuel, is the one I love. But how can I bear this?

She was shaking and she thought she might vomit. Then Rudi's visage came into her mind. "You will do it, Hannah, because you have to. You are strong. This is war. I am not going to die. I am a good pilot."

Taking deep breaths, she sat at her post in a daze. Eventually, her nausea receded and her hands steadied. She was relieved at 1600 hours and went immediately to her hut, climbing under the blankets on her bunk.

Josephs found her there.

"Gluck, what is wrong? Are you ill?"

Hannah was deeply ashamed. "Not feeling quite the thing," she said.

"Me neither," the woman confessed, dabbing her hazel eyes with her handkerchief. She took off her hat and proceeded to take the pins out of her long blonde hair. "I don't know how I can expect myself to endure this day after day. I have no idea whether Luke made it. But I think I would feel it if he didn't make it, wouldn't I? And even if he did crash into the Channel, the odds are he would be picked up, aren't they?"

"I never thought of that," said Hannah, sitting up. "Of course they would be."

Her bunkmate looked at her keenly. "Why *should* you think of that?" Josephs said. "Have you something to tell me, Gluck? Have you got a chap in the RAF, as well?"

She nodded miserably.

"The man who gave you the diamond," Josephs said. "Why didn't you want to say?"

"He's not the man I'm engaged to," she said.

"Oh, dear. Come down here and tell me about it. Something tells me you need to talk it through."

Hannah felt that there was nothing she would like more in that moment than to talk about Rudi. She climbed down from the bunk, keeping the blankets wrapped around her. She couldn't seem to get warm.

"We are both exiles from Vienna," she said, sitting in the canvas folding chair. "Me because I am Jewish, and Rudi because he is the son of an Austrian baron who opposed Hitler. We met in Switzerland after his father was shot by the SS."

Josephs' eyes reflected deepening interest. "Go on," she said.

"We both moved to England and for a while I dated him." Hannah remembered those days, which seemed carefree compared to these. "But my father didn't approve, because Rudi is not Jewish, of course, and so I broke things off."

"But you love him, don't you?"

Hannah looked down at her hands with their long fingers and short fingernails. Rudi loved her hands. "I do. I finally admitted it to myself. But I am engaged to Samuel. It was my father's dearest wish that I marry him. And Papa just died not too long ago."

"This is the twentieth century, Gluck. We don't do arranged marriages anymore. Are you very religious?"

"I'm not. But being a Jew is a racial thing."

"If you listen to Hitler it certainly is. But Western Civilization—the thing we're fighting to preserve—is founded on Judeo-Christian principles. You and Rudi have that in common. It's not like you're an Aborigine. You're not from completely opposing cultures. Does he love you?"

"I think he does," Hannah said with a sigh. "In fact, I'm certain of it, though he's never said so. He doesn't want to put me in an awkward position. In Austria, we could never be legally married, you see. He's a baron. The state church is Roman Catholic. A marriage to a Jew would never be recognized."

"So don't go back to Austria."

Hannah gave her head a little shake. "You make it sound so easy, but Rudi's barony is there. His inheritance. He's fighting this war to get the Nazis out of Austria and reclaim it."

Nellie put a hand on Hannah's shoulder. "Wars inevitably change things. They strip away the dross. I studied modern history at Somerville, Hannah. With the last war, Europe changed, and we will never return to that pseudo-feudalistic state. This war may wipe out the classes altogether. Who knows?"

Hannah took the woman's hand and gave her a little smile. "I thought you were awfully wise. I studied biochemistry at Oxford, but it didn't lend me much real-world wisdom."

Their conversation moved into more general areas as they realized they had a college education in common. While they chattered, Hannah's body eased as tension and fear lessened its hold. They went down to dinner, agreeing that sharing their fears had eased their minds.

Listening to the BBC that evening in the lounge, they heard nothing about RAF losses. The losses on the other side were thought to be considerable—possibly as many as twenty planes.

D

"Care to lay a bet on who is going to win this air war over the Channel?" asked Christian as he met his "friends" at the Boar's Head. He had been thinking of little else, knowing that his brother was flying and in danger.

The red-haired Fromm scoffed. "I won't take your money. The *Messerschmitt* has decimated all of Europe. England is outgunned and outmanned."

Heinemannn added, "There aren't even enough rifles in this country to go around. It would take years for the factories to manufacture the number and type of weapons that will be needed when Hitler invades."

Christian masked his reaction to this defeatist talk. Everything was hanging on the air battle, and he knew it. England must protect the Channel against Goering's huge air force. Clamping down on his fears, he said, "I think you had better keep your voice down."

"I don't understand why the English don't just make peace," Fromm said in low tones. "There is going to be a deadly battle and lots of people are going to cop it."

"The whole world is wondering the same thing, I imagine," said Christian. "I find the English a peculiar people. Do you think America will enter the war on their side?"

"No chance. This is an election year," said Fromm. "Americans have had it with European wars. Even if Roosevelt wished it, he could never convince Congress."

Christian sipped his bitters and wondered if this was true. To him, the future looked very black for England and the rest of Europe.

"Will you go home if it looks like there will be an invasion?" he asked.

The two Americans exchanged looks. "Maybe," Heinemann said. "What will you do?"

Christian swilled his beer and gazed into its depths. "Haven't decided," he said. "I don't know how things are in Detroit or Milwaukee, but in Chicago, we like to back the winner."

His friends raised their pints. "Hear, hear."

Heinemann said in a low voice, "And we all know England can't possibly stand against Hitler alone."

Christian possessed himself in patience, in spite of a desire to press for particulars. He was playing a hunch that the two students were part of a plan, and that they would invite him to participate if he could gain their confidence.

{ 13 }

When he was delivered back to the airfield, Rudi found he was greeted in a mixed manner. His fellow airmen clapped him on the back and congratulated him for the two kills, calling him a "natural ace."

His C.O. however, was less than ecstatic. A hardened man who had seen service in the RAF in the first war, Rudi knew Captain Reynolds was not happy to be commanding an Austrian. "Where's your airplane then, von Schoenenburg?"

"It can be salvaged, sir. It's in a farmyard at present."

"We lost four pilots and their planes today. You almost made it five. Your business is to give it to the enemy and get your plane safely home. We have only about a third the resources that the Jerrys have. We must inflict maximum damage with minimum loss."

"Yes, sir," Rudi said, saluting smartly. Apparently he was to be given no recognition for the kills. But he wasn't looking for commendations. He was looking for revenge. He was looking to wipe the Nazi scourge from the earth.

Retiring to his bunk, he took out a pencil stub and bit of paper and wrote to Hannah:

First day of battle and I downed two MEs. Caught fire but was able to land safely. Took your handkerchief up with me and it obviously brought me luck. This is just the beginning. It is going to be an epic battle, Hannah. I feel it. The men are ready. They are protecting their country from invasion. But you and I know the reality of invasion and I am even more motivated than they are.

At this juncture, I am very glad that we made it to Britain. I am glad both of us were preserved to be part of this fight. My hope is that you are doing well in the WAAFs. I know your work is important.

Please do not worry about me. I am where I want to be, doing what I want to do. All hope that Britain has of deterring an invasion lies with the R.A.F. Without control of the skies over the Channel, the German Navy cannot stage a landing. Our mission in the skies could very well be the turning point for Germany.

Rudi

Hannah was very relieved to receive Rudi's note, but by that time, there had been another air battle. She tried to tell herself that she was engaged in something larger, a grand battle that, as Rudi said, might change the course of the war. She and Rudi were molecules in a grand fighting organism. They must not stop now to consider their fate. Instead, they must work as part of the whole.

The days crawled by. Some days, there were battles; some days the weather prevented them. Hannah became numb. Word traveled down to the Operations Room that Hitler had made a last appeal to the British to surrender. Evidently the Spitfires and the Hurricanes were carrying the message that Britain intended to fight on and foil the rolling forth of the Nazi war machine.

Nika began to see the wounded pilots arrive at Guy's. Most of their injuries were painful burns which they seemed to bear with stoicism. She learned to dress the burns and to add what cheer she could to the ward.

And thus Nika was thrust back into the reality of war. There was nothing that could make it pleasant, but when she was surrounded by men who had given so much and who were bearing it so bravely, she found she could not hold to her private misery. In the common cause in which they fought, it began to unknot itself. She was relieved and energized by the job she had to make things tolerable for these men.

She administered ice baths to stop the burning of their flesh for a little bit while listening to spirited tales of the war over the Channel. She nodded and smiled as she couldn't understand most of what they were saying.

One day, however, a Polish pilot showed up on the ward. He was suffering from burns up one side of his body. Nika lavished attention on him.

"I didn't know Polish pilots were flying in the RAF," she said.

"Oh, yes, ma'am. There are a lot of us, and let me tell you, it is wonderful to be fighting Germans again. The odds are a lot more even in this circumstance."

"Do you really think we can hold them off?"

"I do, actually. I didn't at first. But these RAF chaps are their equal. They really know what they're doing over the Channel. It's a treat to be serving with them."

After the ice bath, she smoothed burn ointment carefully over the affected skin and then wrapped him in bandages. She took heart from the slight hope offered her, even as he suffered his horrible wounds.

"How many pilots are we losing?"

"Not nearly as many as the Germans are. The Spitfires are more maneuverable. Plus fighter command seems to have a miraculous way of sending us right to them. We fly in out of the sun, guns blazing. Problems only come when we let them get higher than we are."

"It makes me feel so good to know our Polish pilots are still fighting them," said Nika. "I have never felt so angry and helpless as I did during the Siege of Warsaw."

"I don't know if you have been in touch with anyone from home, but the Resistance is still fighting the Germans. I don't think they'll give up."

Nika was surprised. "But Warsaw must be completely leveled by now."

"You know what a stubborn lot we Poles can be."

She listened to the tale of the flyer's escape from Poland. When she told him of her own, she felt something comforting settle over her. Was it validation? Hope that maybe their sufferings hadn't been in vain? That they had not given up the fight?

She discussed her feelings with Andrzej that afternoon at tea.

"I know what you mean, Nika. It means a lot to know so many of our fellows escaped. The ones that are not fighting in the air are training with ground troops or being fitted out as undercover agents. Even our government-in-exile is here. Germans and Soviets may be occupying our territory, but we have not given up. We are still a sovereign nation."

Sonia was late that day and did not arrive until after tea. Nika was still so elated by her discovery that her countrymen were not out of the fight, that she spilled her news to her tutor.

"I can see why you would be so happy. From what you have told me, you left behind a country that was steeped in defeat and misery. You brought it here with you. But your eyes are actually sparkling now."

"You see, now I may be able to hope for a good outcome. The RAF fighters I have met are a cheery lot. They seem to think they are holding their own against the Germans."

"I hope they are. The Lord knows I hope they are. And I am glad to see you feeling more optimistic. Life is so much harder when you are miserable."

Nika gave a passing thought to the details of Sonia's life. She had undoubtedly been raised by a selfish and narcissistic mother, yet she seemed sunny and happy.

"How are you settling in with your father?"

"Very well. He isn't home much, but I'm not used to having much time with him at all, so when he is home, I enjoy his company. Now, let us tackle some irregular verbs. Did you memorize the vocabulary I gave you?"

Their lesson proceeded better than usual, and Nika began to hope that she may, eventually, learn English. Sonia was an able teacher.

Halfway through the lesson, there was a tap on the door and Amalia entered.

"Sonia, please stay for dinner. Your father is here, speaking with my husband, and I have invited him to stay also."

The young woman's eyes lit up, and Nika felt a quickening of her heart. It would be good to see Anthony tonight.

After the lesson was over, she indulged herself with a bath in her lavender scented bath salts. Deciding to wear her dark hair down, she curled it with the tongs and brushed it so it fell over one shoulder. She dressed in her only evening gown which she had bought in Paris—a black silk affair with a sweetheart neck and long skirt that flared at the knees. With it she wore the antique silver locket around her neck that she had worn out of Poland. It contained her parents' pictures. After applying red lipstick, powder, and mascara, she examined herself in the mirror.

I'm no siren, but perhaps Anthony is not looking for a siren.

When she walked into the drawing room, he turned to greet her. "My dear, you look sensational," he said.

Nika grew embarrassed. "My one Paris gown," she murmured.

Sonia, standing at her father's elbow, looked at Nika as though she had never properly seen her before. "How lovely," she said, her voice unusually flat.

"Thank you."

Amalia, dressed in a gown of sapphire blue, echoed the compliments. "Nika, you are ravishing, as usual. Would you like sherry or a cocktail?"

"Sherry, please," Nika answered. Turning to Anthony, she said, "Sonia is a good teacher. Thank you so much for arranging for her to teach me."

"She tells me you have an excellent ear, which did not surprise me," he replied. "It is good to see you looking so well."

"I had some good news today." She told him about the Polish flyer and the news of Polish participation in the war which had cheered her. "Our country is not completely vanquished."

"I am glad that made you feel brighter. As a feisty Pole, you must appreciate that all is not lost until we give up."

Tears glazed her eyes as Amalia handed her a glass of sherry. Andrzej smiled at her, his features soft with sympathy. "Your parents would not want you to give up hope. They were very forward-looking."

The tears spilled over and Nika found herself without a handkerchief. Anthony placed his in her hand. "Come now. The darkest hour is before the dawn."

"I am sorry I'm so emotional. I have felt quite frozen up until now."

Amalia spoke. "I know what it's like to lose one's country. But at least yours went down fighting. Mine opened its arms to Hitler."

In that moment, Nika was struck with more admiration for her hostess than ever before. "I cannot imagine your courage, your . . . sacrifice." She did not know how else to refer to the baron's death.

Amalia smiled through her own sudden tears. "I like to think that the war is now taking a turn. I believe Hitler has found his match in the British."

"Hear, hear!" said Anthony. "No more tears, ladies."

Over dinner, during which Nika sat next to Anthony, they discussed the absurdity and pretension of Hitler's "Peace Offer" to Britain during his triumphant speech to the *Reichstag*.

"Duty to his conscience, indeed!" exclaimed Andrzej. "The man is besotted with himself."

"He has no idea the foe he faces in Churchill and the back-bone of the British people," said Anthony. "We will not collapse like France."

"He just thinks if we can accept his new order in Europe, then that will be an end to war," said Amalia. "He has no idea what he is up against. It is not a winding-up scene."

"Is there no faction in Britain that wants to pursue peace on these terms?" asked Nika.

"No one," said Anthony. "Believe it or not. Shilly-shally talk about appeasement is firmly behind us. The government and the people are staunchly in Churchill's camp." He sipped his soup. "And I don't suppose it need be a secret that the Americans have been sending us considerable quantities of weapons across the Atlantic this month. Roosevelt's heart is with Churchill and I have no doubt that he will eventually bring his country around."

During the rest of the meal, Anthony answered questions about President Roosevelt and the Americans. Anthony thought highly of the man, but explained the American political system and the handicaps he and pro-British congressmen faced this election year.

After dinner, everyone retired to the drawing room to listen to the BBC's nightly news broadcast. Anthony sat on one side of Nika, Amalia on the other. As Sonia sat across from her during the broadcast, Nika felt her gaze. Did the daughter object to her friendship with her father?

"It is nine o'clock and this is the BBC reporting from London: The straits of Dover might very well be referred to by the German *Luftwaffe* as 'Hellfire Corner.' Coming from out of the sun, British Spitfires and Hurricane aircraft rain down fire down on the hapless *Messerschmitts.* The shield the RAF provides for Great Britain is far stronger than Reichsmarshal Hermann Goering could ever have predicted. Since what Prime Minister Churchill is referring to as the 'Battle of Britain' began on the tenth of July, over fifty German aircraft have been shot out of the sky by the Royal Air Force who have suffered considerably fewer losses."

Surely fifty aircraft weren't that many out of the huge arsenal the Germans had? Nika felt the tension in Amalia, who sat beside her on the sofa. What would it be like to have a son in the RAF, knowing he was going up, day after day, facing off against the deadly German fighter pilots in their superior numbers? She put a hand over Amalia's and held it tightly. Her hostess looked at her, and Nika read the fear in her eyes. The woman was so brave that Nika tended to forget Rudi's occupation as she nursed his comrades in arms day after day in the hospital. Would they find Rudi among them one day? Or, even worse, would he be shot down to drown in the Channel? Nika thought that perhaps it had been easier when she had felt frozen.

Sonia rose at the conclusion of the broadcast. "I have an early class to teach in the morning. I must get home. Thank you so much for the wonderful dinner, Mrs. Zaleski. Good night, everyone. I will see you at breakfast, Papa."

Amalia and Andrzej accompanied their guest downstairs, while Anthony asked Nika to take a stroll with him in the garden. She agreed and they passed through the French doors onto a terrace and down the steps into the whimsy of a garden that looked brilliant in the late sunset.

"It is rather sobering to think that the future of the war is being determined by young men like Rudi beating off the voracious *Luftwaffe* while we sit back and go about life as usual."

"You are doing good, necessary work at the hospital."

"It is just so odd to have all the action going on at a distance."

"Let us pray that it stays that way, although I really can't imagine that Hitler will hold off bombing London."

Nika took her bottom lip between her teeth.

He continued, "I was thinking tonight at the dinner table that you must think that I am good for nothing except spouting one euphemism after another. Not everyone has the PM's gift with words. But I do think there is reason to be hopeful."

"The British seem to specialize in that." Nika settled herself in a white wrought iron chair overlooking Amalia's rose garden. Their comforting fragrance drifted toward her.

"Zaleski is Polish, and he is one of the most profoundly hopeful people I have ever known."

"I would love to hear how the two of you became such fast friends."

Anthony sat next to her and took out his pipe and tobacco pouch. "I met him in the trenches. He was new to the war, having made his way through the German lines all the way from Vienna."

"Yes, he told me that he fought with the British and French to defeat the Austrian and German empires, so we could have a free Poland. That was very optiminstic of him."

"The incredible thing was that he could take such a risk, knowing he was only one man. It taught me a thing or two. Gave me a new lease on life there in those godforsaken trenches."

"He has always lived by his principles. It is very refreshing."

"At night, we sometimes talked. He told me that he learned to stand for what he believed in from Amalia's uncle."

Intrigued, Nika bade him to continue.

"The uncle was a socialist who inherited a fortune from his father—a wealthy carriage manufacturer who had married the daughter of a count. He could not in good conscience live with all that money. He considered himself 'unequally blessed.' So he gave the money away to charities he chose after close research. And he didn't stop there. He served on their boards to make certain his money was spent in a useful manner. Zaleski said Lorenz Reichart lived the most useful, principled life of anyone he had ever known."

"He sounds very worth knowing. And it would seem that Andrzej has taken his example to heart. He is a very good man. I am so grateful to him and Amalia for taking me in. And they've opened their hearts as well as their home. I don't know what I would have done without them. Most likely, I would be living under Hitler in France." The idea sent a shiver over her.

Anthony lit his pipe and began drawing on it. "Zaleski saved my life in the war. I was knocked out by an explosion once in No Man's Land, and he wouldn't leave me there. He risked his life to carry me back to the trenches on his back. Didn't think twice about it, apparently. Got me to the ambulance and rode with me to the field hospital.

"Then after I suffered the loss of my leg and Madge had left me, he came here on leave. I was not feeling terribly cheery. His robust optimism saw me through that time. He got me out of the house. Walked with me until I was comfortable with my prosthesis."

"That is all of a piece with the man I know," Nika said, remembering when Andrzej had visited her father and talked the politics of democracy late into the night. "I knew our government was doomed when he left the cabinet."

"Speaking of your government, I am organizing a reception for the government-in-exile. It is this Saturday and I require a companion. Would you like to attend? You can be my translator."

"I would be happy to accompany you," she said with a little laugh. "I would not leave you to cope in that wilderness of Polish consonants by yourself."

He put his fingers under her chin. "It's just an excuse to see you," he said softly. "The press of work has been on me day and night, and I've missed you."

"I have been busy myself," she said. "Between my nursing and my English lessons. Sonia gives me fifty vocabulary words to memorize each night, in addition to all those irregular verbs."

"I am glad I was born an Englishman or I probably never would have learned to speak the language." His fingers stroked her cheek. "You really are the most lovely woman."

She smiled softly, her heart tripping along. "It is so peaceful here. You would never know there is a war on, except for that ugly Anderson shelter there at the bottom of the garden."

"Say a prayer for Rudi," Anthony said. "I don't think Amalia could take another death in the family. According to Zaleski, Rudi is the image of his father."

"I shall. She is very brave, isn't she?"

"An incredible woman. Perhaps someday she will confide to you her epic love story. Now, I must go."

Nika had been wanting to kiss him for the last half hour. She rose from her chair as he stood, knocked out his pipe in a nearby planter, and put it in his pocket. He put his hands gently on her shoulders. "You are incredibly brave yourself, Nika."

He brought his face down to hers and kissed her gently and sweetly. Then he took her in his arms and pulled her against his chest. His mouth crushed hers with a hunger she returned. Heart thundering, she put a hand on the nape of his neck, pulling him even closer. Leaving her lips, he kissed the place below her ear and down the side of her neck. A desire she hadn't felt since Bazyli's death welled up inside her like a spring from somewhere deep underground.

Then the thought of her husband and the pain that love could bring caused her to pull away.

"Is anything wrong?" asked Anthony.

"No . . . I just haven't felt anything like this for . . . for a very long time."

"Me neither. It has made me impetuous. But don't fret, my dear. We will take it slowly, if you wish."

"Yes. Yes, that would be good."

"Walk me to the door?"

They shared another kiss in the vestibule, and Nika felt her defenses weakening. His lips caressed her with such warmth and tenderness that she felt her resistance fading. Bazyli had always devoured her like she was a conquest. She felt Anthony's kisses as though they were an offering. His eyes were full of wonder as he gazed down into her face.

"I never thought to feel such things again," he said.

"Nor I," she whispered.

Later as she lay in her bed, she looked back on the evening with feelings of warmth and anticipation. When she left Poland, stripped of family and possessions, full of grief and terrible memories, she never would have believed that, of all things, a new love might await her.

{ 14 }

Christian decided that it was time he stepped up his surveillance of Heinemann and Fromm. If he was correct about their political ambitions, they had to be part of a larger pro-Nazi organization. After all, what could two young American Oxford students do alone in the event of an invasion? Christian would have bet Rudi a fiver that they would soon be in touch with a contact of some sort.

He knew they were studying at St. Edmund's College, and that Friday they had no classes. On that day, he watched from a lookout post across the road from the college doorway. He was gratified when the two students came out at 9 a.m. and headed for the train station. He followed.

As he expected, they boarded the train for London. He took a seat in the next car near the door. He wished he could be close enough to eavesdrop on their conversation, but he dared not risk discovery.

In London, he was first off his car, watching for the red head of Fromm to appear. They went to the taxi queue. Chris grinned. He had always wanted to tell his driver to "follow that cab" like in the American films.

When he did, he witnessed the students' cab disgorge them at The American Café in Piccadilly. They entered the popular spot just in time for elevenses.

Fortunately, the place had its usual crowd. He took a stool at the counter, ordered coffee, and kept a discreet eye on Fromm and Heinemann, who had settled in back at a table for four. They maintained an intense conversation with one another and again, Christian wished he dared to move closer. Perhaps he should have outfitted himself with a disguise.

He was rewarded, however, when a gentleman dressed in a cutaway, striped trousers, and a top hat joined the two. Only government employees of some importance wore rig-outs of that sort. Christian waited until they were deep in conversation, slapped the change for his coffee on the counter and walked through the standing crowd at an angle that gave him full view of the face belonging to the man in the cutaway, all the while keeping himself behind the backs of Heinemann and Fromm. The hair rose on the back of his neck. The Americans had made their disdain for the British and their government clear. Was this man a traitor?

Studying a pocket ABC railway guide, he cast glances at the man until he had memorized his face. There was too much chatter in the restaurant to hear anything at this distance, and he dared not call attention to himself by getting any closer.

When the man rose, Christian followed him at a discreet distance. He watched as the fellow hailed a cab and heard him say to the driver, "The Foreign Office."

At that, Christian hastened away, boarding the first available bus before Heinemann and Fromm could catch him lingering on the pavement. Fortunately, the bus was headed in the direction of the Embankment, his own destination. Pulling out the sketch pad he had thought to bring, he penciled in the face of the man in the cutaway, first using the broad strokes he would use in a caricature and then filling in the fine lines. Fortunately, he had a photographic memory for faces.

When the bus neared the Embankment, he sighted a call box and alighted. Entering the red telephone booth, he rang his boss at MI5.

Half an hour later, he was meeting with the bald and innocuous looking Mr. Braden on a bench on the Embankment. "There's a traitor in the government, I believe." He handed Braden the sketch. "He was meeting with the two Americans, dressed in a cutaway coat and striped trousers. After the meeting, he took a cab to the Foreign Office."

"Hmm," said Braden. "I don't suppose you heard any of their conversation?"

"No. But it was short and intense."

"Sounds ominous," Braden said in a measured voice. "And this face looks familiar to me. I'll ask one or two colleagues. Meanwhile, reinitiate contact with your suspects and see if they make any mention of the meeting."

"Right," said Christian.

"You have my home number. Ring me straightaway if you learn something."

That evening, Christian made his way to the Boar's Head. Heinemann and Fromm were not in evidence. Perhaps they had remained in London to kick up their heels. Disappointed, he nevertheless thought it best to wait through the evening in case they showed themselves. He played some darts and had a pint and a meat pasty at the bar. Excitement was making him grow impatient.

Toward 9 p.m. the two men appeared. Christian kept his head down, showing no outward interest. He felt someone tap him on the shoulder.

"Let me buy you another," said Heinemann. "Come join us."

Christian flashed a grin. "Thought you guys weren't going to show up tonight," he said.

Fromm said, "We've been in London. What've you been up to?"

"Nothing so exciting. Cramming for a quiz I had this afternoon."

After they were settled with their beer, Christian asked, "So what did you do in London? Anything exciting?"

"Depends on what you call exciting," said Heinemann. "We took a tour of the BBC Broadcasting House."

This interested Christian. "I didn't know you were interested in broadcasting."

"It has a lot of possibilities," said Fromm. "The Third Reich has used it to good effect."

"You have to admire the Fuehrer's use of propaganda," Christian said. "Have you seen the film he commissioned— 'Triumph of the Will?' It's amazingly stirring. Gave me goosebumps." Which was the honest truth. Goosebumps of horror.

"So you're an admirer of the Fuehrer, Neuburg?" Fromm pitched his voice low.

"Oh gosh, yes," said Christian, looking around to make certain they weren't overheard. They were sitting in a corner of the dimly lit pub. Most of the patrons were crowded around the darts game. The few who sat at tables were a safe distance away. "I told you. I back winners. He's quite obviously the most compelling world leader in this generation."

The two Americans exchanged looks.

"Would you be willing to go to bat for him?" asked Fromm.

Chris did not have to manufacture his startled look. "You mean join the German army?"

"Not exactly." Fromm glanced around again. "We learned today that Hitler has just issued a new directive. On August fifth, the *Luftwaffe* is to increase their air attack. They're going to start bombing airfields and military installations. This is to be carried out in preparation for invasion, which is now set to occur on August fifteenth."

Christian felt the words like a blow. Could the beleaguered RAF protect this Island against a full onslaught of German might? "How did you come by this information?" he asked.

"Our source is reliable. You can take our word on that."

"What tremendous news. All you hear on the BBC is an account of German losses and claims that Britain is winning the air war," Chris said with perfect truth.

"What would you expect? The invasion is going to come as a complete shock, isn't it?" Heinemann and Fromm grinned broadly and toasted each other.

"Have you ever shot a pistol?" Fromm asked.

"You don't mean you're going to participate in the invasion?" Christian asked with honest surprise.

"Not in the way you think. We have a specific task, and we could use some help. What do you say?"

Privately reeling with the success of his mission as well as the gravity of their news, he manufactured a bit of bravado. "I'm accounted to be a crack shot. I target shoot for recreation when I'm home." They need never know this was false.

"You're just who we need then. We're going to be sent in-structions by coded telegram where to pick up some pistols. And when the invasion takes place, we'll receive another message. We're to go up to London and take down BBC broadcasting house," Fromm said. "Heinemann has broadcasting experience. He's to announce over the air that Great Britain has fallen to the forces of the Third Reich."

Christian was chilled. This had been a pattern employed in Austria during a botched coup by the Germans in 1934. The first thing the military had done was to seize the radio station and broadcast German victory. The coup had failed, but the country had believed for some time that it had succeeded.

"You have been entrusted with such a job?" he asked in-credulously. "You realize if the invasion is turned back that you will be shot?"

Heinemann smiled with confidence. "The invasion will not fail. It will be the same pattern the *Wehrmacht* has employed from Poland to France. How can you doubt that we will suc-ceed?"

"On second thought, you are right to be confident," Christian said, hoping with his whole being that his words would prove false. "And the BBC move is brilliant."

"Can we count you in?" Fromm's visage had changed. His eyes were sharp, his mouth hard. There would be danger in turning him down.

"Of course," he said with manufactured enthusiasm. "It would be an honor."

"That's the spirit!" the Americans said in unison.

"We've been talking it over and we think the best move will be to grab a hostage, first thing," said Fromm.

"It sounds like a plan," said Christian. In reality, he felt ill with dread and was consumed by the need to ring Braden to meet him as soon as possible.

"Another pint to seal the deal," said Heinemann, his narrow face now flushed red with glee.

Chris proceeded to spend the evening until closing time drinking with the Americans. Fortunately, they became drunk enough not to notice that when he got the drinks each time, his own was ginger beer.

Nika was enjoying her English lessons. She would come home after her stint at the hospital, perform a quick wash, change her clothes, and then meet the others for tea. Afterward, she and Sonia would settle into the yellow sitting room for their lesson.

On this particular day, however, Sonia seemed different. She was a bit too bright at tea, her eyes like a bird's darting from one person to another. Giggling, she related an anecdote about the Poles she was teaching, which proved offensive to Nika. She was puzzled at the seeming change in the formerly pleasant Sonia.

When it came time for their private lesson, Sonia sat on the edge of the sofa and looked at her slyly out of the corner of her eye. "You must tell me, Nika, have you a *passion* for my papa?"

Taken aback, Nika didn't know what to answer. She said, "My feelings for your father are my own affair, Sonia."

The woman looked stern. "I like you, Nika, so I had better warn you: he's an unfaithful dog."

Nika felt the words like a slap in the face and instinctively withdrew. "I'm not prepared to discuss the matter with you, Sonia. Perhaps we should skip our lesson today."

"I didn't realize how you felt about him until the other night. I don't want you to get hurt, like my poor mother."

She could hardly credit what she was hearing. Standing up, she said, "I won't listen to any more of this. You shouldn't be discussing these things with me."

"What did he tell you? That my mother left him because of his amputation?"

Nika meant to leave the room, but dread held her there.

"Nothing could be further from the truth," Sonia said. "I love my father, but he is constitutionally unfaithful."

Nika had heard enough. "I don't believe you. Your father was devastated by your mother's affairs." Turning, she left the room.

When she reached her bedroom, she collapsed on the slipper chair. She felt as though Sonia had tried to switch the poles and make north into south. The woman's bitter words couldn't possibly be true.

Staring into space, she went over every conversation she and Anthony had enjoyed in their short acquaintance. Tenderness and compassion had characterized every exchange.

But he was very attractive. Could she believe that he had lived as an unattached bachelor all these years?

Well. Maybe not that. But that he was a womanizer like Bazyli she could *not* believe. No. Sonia was jealous and spiteful. And that raised another problem. Would Anthony choose to pursue their relationship if he knew it was an anathema to Sonia?

The girl had certainly had a difficult enough life, and it seemed father and daughter were at last becoming connected after all these years. Perhaps Nika should pull back. She didn't want to be a source of contention in the family. If she ever fell in love again, she wanted the man's whole heart. She certainly didn't want Anthony to be forced to make a choice between her Sonia.

Sighing, she wondered if she could let Anthony go. She had become attached to him during the past weeks, even though they had seen little of one another. It had seemed that maybe he was the one who could help her to overcome the past and that she could do the same for him. Unexpected pain rose inside her. Her newfound feelings of well being dissolved. She remembered his kiss. Was that the kiss of a womanizer? It was certainly different from Bazily's "take all" ways.

The first kiss had been considerate, tentative, the second verging on unleashed passion. Sensing her withdrawal, he had promised to slow the pace for both their sakes. But life was hard enough at the moment. She didn't need a love affair that was doomed to failure. Her feelings were too raw. It was Anthony who had helped assuage her grief. Perhaps before she became dependent on him, she needed to pull away. She couldn't bear the pain of another loss for whatever reason.

What if Sonia was telling some version of the truth?

When the pub closed at midnight, Christian was able to reach Braden from a telephone box on Carfax after he separated from his drunken companions. His hands were far from steady as he dialed.

"I have vital information. I feel I must meet you immediately, but the last train has left."

Braden said, "I will motor up to Oxford if you feel it to be necessary."

"The war cabinet needs to have this information immediately. I dare not say any more on the telephone."

"I will meet you in the lobby of the Randolph Hotel, where I will make a reservation. It will take me a couple of hours to get there."

Christian went to his room, too anxious to settle to anything. He took a shower, dressed in clothes that didn't smell like cigarettes, and then decided to take a walk.

The darkness was dense, almost palpable. Would Hitler's invasion be successful here as well? Was his symbolic darkness to descend on Oxford, too? Since the thirteenth century, learning had been going on in this place. Could one bully and his fanatic followers bring that all to an end? Would they bomb these golden medieval buildings to rubble?

His soul was so repelled at the idea, he was physically ill. Then he thought of Rudi risking his life each day to keep the Nazis on the other side of the Channel. All the intelligence warned that the *Luftwaffe* was far superior in size to the RAF. Would they just keep coming until all the Spitfires and Hurricanes were shot from the skies? What was to stop them?

He really had the wind up, as the British would say. He needed to stop thinking this way. It was important that they find the traitor in the government. Supposedly, all those with Nazi sympathies had been sacked or reformed. But at least one remained.

If he could enlist the help of the porter at St. Edmund's College, he could intercept any telegrams before they reached Fromm and Heinemann. Yes. They could trace their origin.

At 2 a.m., he made his way to the Randolph Hotel. A clerk remained on duty behind the desk. He explained that he was there to meet Mr. Braden, and took a seat in the posh lobby. It was furnished in modern furniture with a giant portrait of the King over the lighted fireplace.

Braden walked in, nodded at Christian, and, showing the clerk his identification, inquired where they might find some privacy. They were led to a small conference room on the ground floor with floor to ceiling windows, now covered by blackout curtains.

Sitting at the large oak table, Christian waited until the door had closed behind the clerk, and then began his tale. Braden listened intently, his lined face still and grave.

"You're right, von Schoenenburg. I need to get this information to the War Cabinet immediately. I don't know if Hitler's going to pull this off, or whether he's delusional, but we need to be prepared."

Christian told his boss of his intention of intercepting the telegrams.

"Jolly good idea. Let us know when and where they're to pick up their weapons and we'll meet them with a warrant for their arrest for conspiracy to overthrow the government. I'll send a stenographer tomorrow to take down your statement. We'll arrange for it to be done here in this room with a guard at the door so that it will be completely secret."

"I'll have to check with the porter at St. Edmund's several times a day. I don't have a private telephone."

"Try to check in every hour," Braden advised. "I've shown your sketch to Lord Halifax in the Foreign Office and I have a tentative identification. The telegram should confirm that our traitor is from there. If our guess is right, you'll have to positively identify him before we can get a warrant to search his office and his home."

"As soon as the telegram about the pistols comes, I will ring you and we can go from there."

"We will probably include you in the arrest, so as not to tip our hand if anyone is observing from a distance."

"I'll be prepared," Christian said.

{ 15 }

Anthony called for Nika and the Zaleskis for their evening out at the home of Lord Halifax where they were to attend the reception for the Polish Government-in-Exile. Aside from Nika's company, he was not looking forward to it. There was too much ill feeling between the members of the Polish government.

Zaleski voiced this same concern as they motored to the Foreign Minister's house nearby in Mayfair. "Things do not appear to have altered much in the government since I left it. The names have changed, but the bickering is the same."

"For what should I prepare myself?" asked Nika.

"My cousin, August Zaleski, the Foreign Secretary, is in conflict with Prime Minister Sikorski over relations with the Soviet Union and has been ever since the Russians invaded," said Andrzej. "I shouldn't say anything further, I suppose."

"Halifax has been approached in the matter," Anthony said. "No doubt it will be discussed tonight. We might as well inform Nika and Amalia of the situation."

"As you wish," Andrzej said. "Sikorski wants Churchill to broker a treaty between the Soviet Union and Poland whereby the Soviets would end their deportations of Polish citizens and their reign of terror in Poland. Though the Soviets are at peace with Germany, Sikorski feels this is only a temporary situation. He wants to raise an army of three hundred thousand Poles to fight the Germans. It's all very previous, and doesn't serve either Britain's or the Soviet interests at the moment. The British have their hands full and don't particularly want to alienate Russia. My cousin will have nothing to do with any kind of deal to do with the Soviets."

"Do *you* feel the peace between Stalin and Hitler to be temporary?" asked Amalia.

"Absolutely," answered Anthony. "Now we are here. Let us put on our happy faces."

Anthony was very glad he brought Nika. Halifax's eyes brightened as he was introduced to her in the receiving line. Elegant in her black evening gown with her hair dressed high on her head, she greeted the Foreign Secretary in French.

Anthony said, also in French, "Mrs. Kochanski is a citizen of Warsaw who escaped through Hungary to France and then here. She lost all of her family and is residing with the Andrzej Zaleskis. She will be teaching at Somerville College in the fall term."

Halifax said, "I offer you my sincere condolences on the deaths of your family, Mrs. Kochanski. I welcome you to our home. Do you know any of the Polish cabinet ministers?"

"I am acquainted with Foreign Secretary Zaleski through his cousin," Nika said.

Lord Halifax nodded. "A man of sound views, I believe."

As they moved past the Foreign Secretary, Nika raised an eyebrow at Anthony. "I guess we know where he stands," she whispered.

"Ah, but whether he was talking about Andrzej or August is the question."

Prime Minister Sikorski, a short balding man, was interested to meet Nika. Anthony did not understand their conversation, but afterward she told him that the man had apparently known her father and she had informed him of his death and that of her mother and brother. He had vowed to seek justice for all the Poles who had died at the hands of their enemies.

Nika translated for him most of the evening. The talk was all speculation about how long it would be before the Nazi-Soviet Pact would be broken by Hitler attacking Russia through Poland. Anthony felt as though he were suddenly part of a different war. No one seemed to care about what was going on in the Channel or whether there would be an invasion.

He found himself agreeing with Zaleski's assessment of the Polish government. This had the effect of making him very glad for the united front the British were operating under at the moment.

At close to eleven o'clock, Halifax pulled him aside and took him into his library.

"We have a potential problem, Fotheringill. MI5 has identified Nigel Reston meeting with two American pro-Nazi sympathizers. We know nothing more than that now. I realize you have known the man since the last war. What do you think? Is he solid, or could there be something to this?"

Shock jolted through Anthony making him temporarily mute. Was Halifax saying Reston was a traitor? Impossible!

He scoffed at the suggestion his friend was cozy with the Nazis. "There is some innocent explanation, I'm sure. Reston is not a great fan of Churchill, but other than that, he is solid. He fought the Germans in the last war! Who are these Americans?"

"Oxford students. MI6 is looking into their origins. MI5 is keeping an eye on them. We should know more soon. In the meantime, any untoward behavior or conversations you witness should be reported directly to me."

"Yes, sir."

"Now let us get back to our guests."

The seed of suspicion had been sown, however. Anthony was preoccupied the rest of the evening trying to recall all his recent discussions with Reston. He was aware that Nika noticed it.

When they returned to The Laurels, she asked him if he was worried about something.

"Nothing I can discuss, I'm afraid. Sorry if I've seemed distant."

She hesitated, then asked him to accompany her into the downstairs sitting room. "There is something we need to discuss, Anthony."

He returned immediately to the present. "Of course."

She sat on a chair, eliminating the possibility that they might have a tête-à-tête on the sofa.

"Anthony, first of all, you have been most kind to me since I have come to London."

Dash it! This didn't sound promising. "Any kindness I may have shown was spurred by sincere admiration, Nika."

"Thank you. But that just makes what I have to say more difficult."

He waited.

"I'm not ready for a romance. I have scars you know nothing about, and they run deep. I would like for us to just remain friends."

He felt as though he were a balloon that had just been punctured. He had difficulty believing this was the same woman who had kissed him so passionately just the other night. "What has happened, Nika? What has made you change your mind? I have a great deal of difficulty believing that you kiss your friends the way you kissed me."

He watched her blush fiery red.

"Yes, well, that was a slip-up. I never said I don't find you extremely attractive."

"Something has happened," he insisted.

"I just think it's poor timing. For both of us. It's wartime. Emotions are running high. I don't want to make a mistake."

"I think wartime merely strips away pretense. I believe it clarifies things. Shows us what is most important. You are important to me, Nika. Not in an ephemeral sense. It's more than that. I'm not looking for a fling."

Her eyes pleaded with him. "Please, Anthony. Don't make this more difficult."

"It is you who are raising the difficulties." He smiled at her, full of tenderness at her vulnerability. "I can be patient, Nika. You are worth it."

Dear Hannah,

I know I am tired, but I am so wired with tension that it is impossible to relax. Fortunately, there have been several days where the weather was so bad over the Channel that we haven't had to fly every single day. But on the days I don't fly, I wish I were in the air, for doing nothing is difficult.

After the first few days of the battle, I stopped trying to have anything but the most superficial relationship with the other pilots. My good friend William was shot down. I don't know if he is dead or taken prisoner by the Germans. Not knowing is difficult. It is better to live in light camaraderie—playing darts or cards with the other pilots, but keeping one's thoughts to oneself.

Leaving the airfield is prohibited, even on foggy days, lest the fog should suddenly dissipate and the call to scramble be issued. Everything before this battle seems to be a haze of distant memory.

Everything but you. Your handkerchief goes up with me every time. That probably seems silly, but it has become my talisman—my reminder that there is another life. Another life that contains you.

I have little to say, because my whole present now is this battle. I won't bore you with details, but it just seems to go on and on until I think it will never end.

Yours always,

Rudi.

He sealed and addressed the letter, then went back to trying to read a magazine about fishing, which had never held the least bit of interest for him. He could have told her that he had shot down five planes, including the two he had shot down on the first day. This was enough to make him a "jolly good shot." He now flew point in the formations and made certain that his Spitfire stayed high. The great advantage the enemy had over them was that the Messerschmitt could gain height more rapidly than the RAF planes.

But he didn't really think she would be interested in that.

Hannah was grateful for the news that Rudi sent, but wished he would write more details about the battle. It struck her to the heart that the flyers didn't dare to make close friendships. She wished so much she could be with him or at least write to him. She longed to give him support and comfort.

Her own work was becoming more routine. She found she was able to distance herself from the true meaning of the dots she saw on radar and the blocks on the plotters table.

There were foggy days when there were no battles, and she had taken to reading Agatha Christie mysteries on the job. She had never been a great reader of popular fiction, but Nellie Josephs had convinced her that mysteries were just the thing—engaging and neat and tidy with just desserts coming to the villains. Soon she was branching out to Dorothy L. Sayers and Margery Allingham as well.

There was electricity in the air, however. Everyone sensed that sooner or later the Germans were going to lose patience with the dogfights and were going to risk sending massive numbers of bombers so that enough would get through to do serious damage. As anxiety built up in Fighter Command headquarters, Hannah began almost to wish that the day would come so that at least they would know what they were up against and could do something about it.

Once they had seen Christian's credentials, the porters at St. Edmund's College had promised to hold back any telegrams for Mr. Heinemann or Mr. Fromm until Chris had a chance to inspect them. After giving his deposition to the MI5 stenographer whom he met at the Randolph, he made hourly calls from the box outside his own college. He gave up any pretense of being a dedicated student, neglecting his lectures.

On the second day, Mr. Jenkins, porter at St. Edmund's, informed him that the expected telegram had come. Praying that neither of the Americans would see him, he visited the porter's lodge and took temporary possession of the message. Using the electric teakettle Jenkins kept for his tea, they steamed the telegram open. Christian saw that the point of origin for the telegram was designated as the Foreign Office, London. The signature was coded. He copied the entire message into his sketchbook and then resealed the telegram.

After thanking Jenkins, he walked away from the college down onto Broad Street, dodging cars, bicycles, and double decker buses, until he found a telephone box. Placing the trunk call to Braden, he read the coded message exactly as it was written, including the spaces. There were people at MI5 who specialized in decoding such things. Christian knew he could do it himself, but they would be quicker, and time was of the essence.

"The Foreign Office, eh?" said Braden. "That confirms our suspicions. Look sharp tonight, and I'll see you at the drop."

Christian rang off. That evening, he met his supposed comrades in the Boar's Head.

"We've got the location of the pistols," said Heinemann. "They're to be dropped in a dust bin at the train station tonight. If the three of us go, two can act as a screen while the other one of us picks them out of the bin. They're coming on the last train—ten-thirty pm."

Christian thought quickly. He needed to let Braden know at once.

"Good news," Chris responded. "I'll meet you there, if that's all right. I've got an interview with my tutor tonight. It's important for us to keep up normal appearances."

Fromm looked at him as though he were crazed. "Do you think you're being watched or something?"

"I just think we should be as careful as possible," Chris said. "People are paranoid about what they call Fifth Columnists. What if someone *is* watching us?"

Fortunately, Heinemann seemed to buy it. It probably appealed to his sense of the dramatic. "Perhaps we had better split up now and meet at the train station. It's the dust bin by platform six, just as you enter the main station from the trains. We'll meet at ten-thirty precisely."

They left the pub. Christian left first, ducking into a doorway until the other two men had passed, one at a time. He saw them go in separate directions. In case one of them got suspicious and doubled back to follow him, he went off to his room in Christ Church College. His palms were sweating with nerves.

Did they believe him? Were they watching, waiting to see what he did? He looked at his watch. 7:30. He only had three hours until the drop. *This is it.* This was what he had trained for, and it was an enormous responsibility to carry it through successfully.

Act normally. He would have to take a chance on his tutor. Taking his class notes with him, he started off to call on his Plato tutor, Dr. Grimes. He knew he lived in rooms next to his office. Walking briskly, he knocked on the tutor's door fifteen minutes later.

When Dr. Grimes recognized him, his eyebrows jumped up near where his hairline would have been if he were not completely bald.

Christian said, "I have a bit of a problem, sir." He showed his MI5 credentials. "I may be being followed, and I have to ring my boss immediately. Do you have a telephone?"

"Er . . . yes. I do," said his tutor. "Come right in Mr. Neuburg."

He led him to his desk.

"It's a trunk call to London. I'll have to reimburse you."

"That will not be a problem."

Christian made his call. After he had given Braden the information, his boss said, "This will be a full operation. Several agents will be there. We will arrest you, as well, as we discussed."

"Any luck on tracing the Foreign Office contact?"

"The name was a pseudonym, we think. So your sketch is our only clue, and we can't link that conversation you saw specifically to a briefing about the planned operation at the BBC. Perhaps the young men will talk with some persuasion."

"Let's hope so," said Christian, feeling a bit deflated.

After the telephone call, Christian thanked Dr. Grimes. "Would you mind if I stayed a bit? I won't get in your hair. It's just that I'm meant to be having a meeting with you. That's my cover."

"I don't suppose you can tell me about it?"

"Sorry, sir."

"That's all right. I'm glad to have been of service."

{ 16 }

When Anthony returned to his office after lunch, his secretary informed him that Mr. Roger Braden of MI5 was awaiting him in his office. Annoyed, he realized this must be about the Reston matter Lord Halifax had spoken to him about the other night.

He supposed he needed to listen to the man. Walking into the room, he extended his hand.

"Mr. Braden? Anthony Fotheringill. How may I be of service?"

His visitor rose and shook his hand. A man of medium height and weight, he had a head of heavy iron gray hair and a lined face that wore an air of gravity. He walked to the door and shut it.

"Mr. Fotheringill, I am investigating a serious matter. I understand that Lord Halifax has spoken to you?"

"Yes. About Nigel Reston. I told him the whole thing had to be a mistake. I've known the man for years. We were at Oxford together after the war."

"I understand from Lord Halifax that you also know a young man by the name of Christian von Schoenenburg? That he used to live with you, as a matter of fact?"

"Of course. Don't tell me he's under suspicion, too. I absolutely refuse to believe that."

Braden cleared his throat. "As a matter of fact, he works for me. It was he who made this sketch. I'd like you to take a look at it."

He handed Anthony a piece of paper. Studying it carefully, his spirits took a dive. "I'd say he'd got Reston's likeness to the life. Where did he see him?"

"Von Schoenenburg has been undercover at Oxford. He has met two Americans whose families are known to be great supporters of the Nazi cause. The young men, a Mr. Heinemann and a Mr. Fromm are engaged in a conspiracy to overthrow the government upon a supposed Nazi invasion. They have been told this will take place near the fifteenth of August." Braden paused, getting to his feet and paced the length of the room like a panther. Anthony felt the impact of his words. The date was only two weeks away. "They take their orders from a man in the Foreign Office. They were seen meeting with Mr. Reston at the American Café in Piccadilly. That evening they recruited von Schoenenburg to work with them to make an armed assault on the BBC the day of the supposed invasion and seize control. They are meant to broadcast that the government has fallen to the Nazis."

Braden paused, and Anthony knew he was letting his words settle in. The whole thing was diabolical. The MI5 operative continued, "Today arrangements have been made for them to take delivery on a cache of pistols that will be concealed in the Oxford train station. Our men will take them into custody. However, Fromm and Heinemann know their leader by a pseudonym only."

Anthony grew progressively colder. Braden's suspicions of Reston were well reasoned and logical. "I'm sorry, but I find it very difficult to believe that Reston would engage in subversive activities against this country."

"There is always the chance that he is being blackmailed. Does he have any family in Germany?"

Anthony started to answer in the negative, but suddenly remembered a fact he had long forgotten. "His sister. She went to school in Heidelberg and married a German. He has been to visit her a number of times. They were very close growing up, as their parents died young."

"Do you know her politics?"

"No. He has never mentioned them."

Braden leaned back in his chair. "Ah." He sat and crossed his legs as though he were finally getting comfortable. "Then we have two possible scenarios, don't we? Either she and her family are being held hostage by the Nazis or Reston has become a Nazi himself at some juncture."

Anthony contemplated these possibilities with growing alarm. Unbidden, Reston's recent criticisms of Churchill and the British war effort came to mind. "I believe he did think we should pursue some kind of compromise with Hitler."

Braden nodded, but his forehead was furrowed. "If these Americans choose, they can identify Reston as their contact within the conspiracy. But if they won't, even if von Schoenenburg identifies him as the man in the café, we will have a difficult time pinning anything on him without further evidence. What you have told me about his sister, however, gives me grounds for a warrant to search his office and residence.

"Somehow, he is in contact with someone who is privy to Hitler's most recent directives. The easiest way would be by shortwave radio."

Anthony ran a hand over his scalp and gripped the back of his neck with his palm. His mind kept playing scenes from the Oxford days and all the camaraderie he and his friend had enjoyed since that time. But Braden's case seemed solid. There was really very little chance that he was wrong. "I am beginning to see that you must be right. But if you arrest his American minions, he may panic and get rid of any evidence."

"That is why we must move tonight, before he hears anything. Your information about his sister has been a great help. Somehow, it slipped through the cracks. Halifax had no knowledge of it."

"That in itself is ominous, I suppose."

Braden got to his feet. "I think so."

𝒟

Christian arrived at the drop at ten-thirty as planned. He met Heinemann and Fromm who were sitting on a bench outside Platform Six.

"Any more communications?" Christian asked.

"Nothing," said Fromm. "As far as we know everything is still a go." He chewed the fingernails on his left hand.

Heinemann ran both hands over his head through his thick blond hair. "It's ten-thirty. I say we go for it."

They had no difficulty finding the dust bin. Fromm and Christian positioned themselves around it while Heinemann fished inside. He lifted a paper bag and checked inside. "We're set."

At that moment, four men in dark trench coats and hats moved out of the shadows. "You're set, all right," the man Christian recognized as Braden said. The other three men moved in and handcuffed all three students in the blink of an eye.

"Hey! What's going on here?" Heinemann asked, tossing the bag back into the dust bin in spite of the handcuffs. "What do you think you're doing?"

Braden pronounced, "Mr. Randolph Heinemann, Mr. David Fromm, and Mr. Christian Neuburg, I arrest you all on charges of conspiracy to overthrow His Majesty's Government in time of war. The penalty, I am afraid, is death."

The MI5 operative retrieved the bag containing the pistols. His minions shoved the three young men in the back, moving them forward out of the train station.

"Who gave us away?" Fromm demanded. "How did you know?"

"You have been under surveillance for some time. Your disdain for Britain is quite evident," Braden said.

"There won't be a Britain for much longer," spat an angry Heinemann. "Hitler is going to come down on you like a million tons of steel."

"Then I guess we had better hang you quickly," Braden replied.

Christian did not enjoy his night in custody. All three of them were put together in a bleak concrete cell with two guards standing outside.

"Do you think we'll really be put to death?" Fromm asked his cohorts.

"We were found in the thick of a conspiracy to commit treason," Heinemann said. "Our parents need to know about this. Perhaps they can help."

"What about your contact?" Christian asked. "Is he in any position to help you out?"

"Not without revealing his identity. It would look fishy if he took an interest in three American kids."

"Maybe you can work out a plea," Chris suggested. "You could identify him in exchange for a lighter sentence."

"That's a good idea," said Fromm with enthusiasm. "Why should we die because of European politics?"

Chris simmered with the thought that they had been eager enough to stab England in the back.

Heinemann said, "I don't know, Fromm. That seems wrong."

"Do you want to be hanged?" demanded the redhead, his face flushed.

Fingering his throat, the rangy American said, "We would have to secure the promise in writing. What we need is a lawyer."

"I hope you'll put in a good word for me," Chris said, managing to infest his words with gloom.

"We don't even know his real name," Fromm said, suddenly discouraged. "Just that he holds a high post in the government."

"Have you ever met him in person?" Christian asked.

"Several times," Heinemann said. "Mostly before the war."

"How in the world did you ever meet him?" Christian wanted to know.

"He actually came to the Boar's Head a few times. Before the war, when there were German students there still. We became acquainted through his son."

"His son?" Chris tried to keep the enthusiasm out of his voice.

"Yes. Werner was raised in Germany by his mother's parents," Heinemann said. "She died when he was born. His parents were never married, and he went by his mother's last name." Heinemann ran his hands through his hair again. "Our contact, Werner's father, called himself by Werner's last name when he was with us, but we later found out he was using it as an alias. Werner would never tell us his English name. They had it planned way back then that he would be a 'sleeper agent' for Hitler in the government."

Fromm interjected, "He knows Hitler personally. From as far back as his Munich days."

Christian hoped that the guard outside their cell was getting all of this. "So Werner is now fighting for Hitler, I presume?"

"*Luftwaffe,*" said Fromm. "His father is very proud."

"Well, I think you were set up," Chris said, intentionally fanning the flames. "You do need a lawyer. Only here, they call them solicitors."

When Braden let himself into their cell at one in the morning, Heinemann asked for a solicitor before the MI5 agent could ask his first question.

"We want a deal," he said. "We have a contact high in your government. We will identify him for you if we can have the death penalty revoked."

"Conspirators to overthrow Her Majesty's Government are not entitled to solicitors. However, perhaps we can work something out between us?" Braden suggested, his voice like silk. Christian had never heard him speak so softly.

"Like what?" asked Fromm.

"You give us a statement and I will put in a good word for leniency. It is the only chance you have, frankly. I would advise you to take it."

Christian looked back and forth between his boss and the two men whose brows had fallen in despair. He thought that they were just now beginning to comprehend their fates.

"I would like to give a statement," Fromm said.

"As would I," Heinemann added.

"I will take your statements separately while you are isolated from each other. "What about you, Neuburg?"

"I will make a statement also," Chris said. With difficulty, he kept his elation to himself.

Hours later, Christian was called into the interrogation room, the last to give his "statement."

Braden didn't waste a moment. "We've got him. Both men recognized Reston, an undersecretary in the Foreign Office, from your sketch. They told us the whole story of how they were recruited, together with the interesting news that Reston has an illegitimate German son."

"Good," said Christian. "When will you make the arrest?"

"Now," said Braden. "Top notch work, von Schoenenburg. You've caught a very nasty traitor."

"What now?" he asked.

"The youngsters will make a formal identification of Nigel Reston, then I will suggest some form of clemency for them, but I have no idea if it will be granted. I am keeping them in solitary confinement so they will not know that you have been set free. I have another important job for you. Get some sleep and then meet me at Mr. Reston's residence—7 Cheyne Walk in Kensington at noon. We found Reston's shortwave radio."

Christian agreed but doubted that he could sleep after all the excitement of the night.

Lord Halifax called a meeting on August 2nd of all the undersecretaries. Anthony's heart was heavy as he went into the conference room. He had no doubt of what the subject was they would discuss.

He was right.

"Gentlemen, I have a grave matter to present to you. Our colleague, Mr. Reston, was arrested for treason in the early hours of this morning. I do not need to tell you the sordid details. The Prime Minister has asked that we do not discuss it among ourselves. It will not be covered by the Press. Such a story would reflect very poorly indeed upon the credibility of the Foreign Office.

"What I am asking now is that if any of you have any details you have observed about Mr. Reston which might be deemed as suspicious—contacts he had within the government, etcetera—please speak with me privately and I will arrange for you to meet with MI5. This traitor has been in place in our government for many years, and we don't know the extent of the damage he might have done. He had a family in Germany of whom we were completely unaware. We are anxious to discover the depth and breadth of his culpability."

Anthony was grateful he had had some advance preparation of this news, for the reality of it took his breath away. That he could have associated with a man living a double life for so many years and not detect anything was almost unimaginable. His confidence in his own judgement was knocked askew and fractured right up the middle. Was he himself suspect as a known associate of Reston?

The meeting was dismissed and he walked slowly back to his office. *I should have known. I should have guessed somehow. All those trips to Germany. His hostility toward Churchill. But who suspects a man one thinks is among one's closest friends?*

Anthony wished for once that, like some of his colleagues, he kept a flask of brandy in his office. Things like this made one question one's whole version of reality.

{ 17 }

The pilots stationed at Biggin Hill Field were called together the morning of August 3rd. Captain Reynolds paced the area in front of the briefing room as he spoke.

"We have received intelligence that Jerry is gearing up for invasion. He has been relatively quiet lately with the bad weather, but he is ready to stage an all-out assault, sending large numbers of bombers across the Channel, taking the chance that some of them will get through. He will concentrate on our air fields and all our military installations. He may even get as far as London.

"We have a large task ahead of us. We are somewhat outnumbered, as you know. However, the bombers are easier targets than the *Messerschmitts*. Be alert to opportunities to dodge the escorts and target the bombers. These attacks are to ensue as soon as the weather is propitious. At this point Jerry hopes to invade on August fifteenth.

"It will be an epic fight, gentlemen. But if we have anything to say about it, an invasion of our Island will not take place on August fifteenth or any other day!"

This challenge awoke Rudi again to his purpose. Determination stirred within him. It was more than just the never ending dogfights. They had a direct challenge to face. The fate of England truly hung in the balance.

Hannah received a letter from Samuel the same day they learned that there was a big German attack brewing sometime during the next few days. It was an unfortunate juxtaposition.

Dearest Hannah,

I am growing very weary of this separation. I hope that you will be able to arrange leave soon.

Life at Oxford proceeds slowly. As you know the summer term is mostly for foreign students. Even if it weren't, there wouldn't be many British students, as they are all in the army or the RAF. We have received word of many deaths of our scholars both in France and over the Channel. I can't help but wonder what cause can be so dire that it would cost all these lives. And I fear it has just begun.

Surely there will be an invasion, and with Churchill's attitude, Britain will not go quietly, but will fight to the last man. The whole idea sickens me.

I know we differ on this subject, but surely you can see that the sacrifice of so many lives is an outrage to humanity.

I hope we will be able to see one another soon.

With all my love,

Samuel

Hannah tore the letter to shreds and burned it in her anger. How could a scholar of philosophy be so terribly blind to the danger Hitler and his Aryan beliefs presented? One would suppose that a thinker of any depth would see that a man who burned books and exercised totalitarian control over the subjects "acceptable" to the Reich, not to mention his treatment of the Jews, must be stopped. Rudi was in the skies every day, risking his life for his beliefs while Samuel remained in his Ivory Tower saying it was all meaningless.

She could not bear the dichotomy. It was too much. Taking out pen and paper, she wrote the letter that should have been written before now.

Samuel,

Our views of life are so divergent that I cannot see how we ever thought of being married. I am sorry if this causes you pain, but please consider our engagement at an end. I cannot possibly marry you.

Hannah

Once she had mailed the letter, she felt an immense weight lift from her soul. How long had she known this would never work? She had clung to it because it was what Papa wanted, but each day that the war advanced, she was more enmeshed in the cause. She couldn't imagine ever being married to anyone who did not feel as wholeheartedly committed as she was. Now she felt amazingly free.

She confided the whole story to Josephs, and they celebrated with drinks at the local pub.

"Does this mean you will marry your pilot?" her friend asked.

"I didn't do this because of Rudi. I broke the engagement because Samuel and I are completely incompatible. For a philosophy professor, he is totally blind to the threat of Hitler. He all but ridiculed those who were fighting. How I ever thought we had enough in common to marry is a complete mystery to me."

"It is to me, too," said Josephs. "How did it come about?"

Hannah twisted her glass in her hands, remembering those days, which seemed so far off now. "He and my father were friends. Papa wanted me to marry a good Jewish man. They talked philosophy into the wee hours. But I am now convinced that had he really understood Samuel's beliefs about this war, he would never have wanted me to marry him. If there was one thing Papa understood, it was Hitler's anti-Semitism. That is the whole reason we sought refuge in England."

"I am glad you have come to your senses."

Hannah gave her a wry smile. "Samuel is very good looking."

"Were you more attracted to him or to Rudi?"

Thinking of the current that had flowed between her and Rudi at their good-bye, she said, "Rudi. It has always been Rudi. Ever since I first met him by the lake in Zürich."

"And what about the religion problem? How do you feel about that now?"

"Rudi has to survive the battle, Josephs." Tears sprang to her eyes. "And I am not at all sure that I should count on that happening."

Her friend covered Hannah's hand with her own and gave it a squeeze. "I know, darling. Believe me, I know."

$\mathcal{D}$

Nika was not surprised when Sonia failed to show up for her English tutoring after their last acrimonious session. Not knowing how she would face the young woman, she was somewhat glad that she didn't come.

Amalia commented on her absence at tea. "What has become of Sonia, I wonder?"

"We had some unfortunate words the last time she was here. She tried to convince me that Anthony was a Don Juan and that he would break my heart."

"Really? How dreadful," Amalia said as she buttered her toast. "She must be afraid of losing him to you. Anyone less of a Don Juan than Anthony, I have yet to meet."

"She played to my insecurities, though she couldn't have known it. And I am loath to come between Sonia and her father."

"Does this mean you are going to discourage him? I hope not. Both of you deserve some happiness, Nika. And I believe he genuinely cares about you."

"You don't think there could be any truth in what Sonia says? How well do you know him? I know he and Andrzej are close."

"I think I know him quite well. We lived with him for about six months when we first came to England. During that time, I wasn't aware of any women in his life. He was still married then, and I think he took his vows seriously—though Madge certainly didn't."

"I was very deceived in my husband," Nika explained. "I don't think I have ever really gotten past it. There hasn't been another man in my life since Bazyli." Nika took a bite of toast before going on. "Add that to the fact that I am very aware of my own vulnerability just now. I don't think it is the right time for me to get involved with anyone."

"Well," said Amalia, "you know best, of course. But there was never a kinder man than Anthony."

Nika pondered those words that night as she lay in bed, waiting for the bombs to begin falling as she did every night. She tried to ward off these fears with thoughts of Anthony's face which had become dear to her. Was she going to let past pain cause her to throw away any chance of further happiness?

Instead of answering the question, her mind overcame her with her night terrors: the Stuka bombers with their horrid whistling sound just before they exploded, spreading death and devastation; her dear mother lying pinned under the beam, her eyes glazed with death; the blood and the horror in the streets as she went out to try to find food.

How long before London was another Warsaw?

Anthony longed to confide his self-doubt to someone, but was prohibited from doing so by the direct order from Churchill. He arrived home late, as usual, and was very glad Sonia was there to greet him. She and Cook managed to make do very well with the rations, and a hearty stew was awaiting him.

He hated to think what life on this Island would be without the Royal Navy guaranteeing the delivery of foodstuffs. There wasn't enough farmland or farm stock to begin to feed the inhabitants of the Island. One of the many reasons it was important for the RAF to succeed was to keep their lines of supply open on the sea.

"You look more weary than usual, Papa," his daughter commented.

"It was a bad day," he admitted. "This is very good stew, however, and it is wonderful to have someone to come home to."

"Anything you can talk about?"

"Nothing, except to say that my faith in a man I thought I knew well was completely shattered. It has shaken me, rather."

"You always think the best of people," she said. "Even Mum, when she certainly didn't deserve it."

"For pity's sake, Sonia. The last thing I need to discuss now is your mother."

"I'm sorry. What would you like to talk about?"

He broke his dinner roll and spread it with homemade apricot jam from the estate in Wiltshire. "You. How is your tutoring going?"

"Very well. The Poles and the Belgians are eager to learn, and that helps. Now that the Norwegian government-in-exile has moved here, I have some of them, as well."

"And Nika? How is she doing?"

When she did not answer immediately, Anthony looked up from his meal and studied her face. She was biting her bottom lip, the picture of uncertainty.

"What is it, darling?"

"We had a disagreement. I have decided it is too uncomfortable to continue tutoring her. I'm sorry. I know you particularly wanted me to help her."

"A disagreement?" He was astonished.

She paused before answering, crumbling her roll into her stew.

"I really would prefer not to discuss it. I know how you feel about her. You're in love with her, aren't you?"

Anthony started at the bold question. "What makes you say that?"

"That old line from the romance novels: 'I've seen the way you look at her.'"

He certainly didn't intend to discuss his most private feelings. "We're taking things slowly, Sonia. We've both been badly burned."

"I think I should warn you, Papa. Nika is not at all what she seems."

After the revelations about Reston, these words were the last thing he needed to hear. "And what do you mean by that, Sonia?"

"I won't say anymore. I just want you to be careful. You don't deserve to be hurt again."

Anthony grew annoyed. "Let me worry about that, Sonia. And I would thank you for not meddling in my affairs."

The rest of the meal was spent in uncomfortable silence. After the BBC evening news, he shut himself up in his library.

What did Sonia mean when she said Nika was not all that she seemed? The poor woman was like a wounded animal and he had thought he was finally reaching inside her protective shell. To him, she seemed kind and good.

But then, he hadn't thought Reston was a traitor, either. Perhaps he should cool things down a bit. But he didn't want to keep his distance. Every instinct bade him to cherish Nika, to make her feel warm and secure.

That thought sent him off on another tangent. He was foolish to think he could offer anyone security as long as the maniac Hitler raged through the world. He knew all hell was about to break loose.

{ 18 }

Christian found Reston's flat to be modern—a study in chrome and black glass with black leather furniture. It made him feel cold. The shortwave radio was in the bedroom, set up on a glass table under the window. The problem was going to be that he didn't know the pass code.

He set about looking for anything that might help him. Nigel Reston had been arrested completely unexpectedly, so he would not have had time to have destroyed any records. Chris searched the desktop cabinet without much hope. He found only stationery supplies. The bedside table held nothing. Nor was there anything in the wardrobe or the chest of drawers.

He spread out his search into the sitting room and the kitchen, where he found nothing. The last room to search was the bathroom. In the medicine cabinet, he found a small pillbox with a prescription label. It felt light and empty, but when he opened it, there was a scroll of silk fabric. When he unrolled it, he took a deep breath and grinned. It was only the width of the pillbox, but it was long. A string of dates was written in black ink on the left hand side. In the right column were letters and numbers. He hoped they were the access codes for that day.

When would Reston have sent and received transmissions? The best guess was early morning before he went to work at the Foreign Office, or sometime in the evening. Chris knew he would only have one shot at initial contact. It was now afternoon. He would wait by the radio and hope that the German contact would make the first transmission.

Growing weary and hungry by early evening, he unpacked his meal. It was scarcely worth the name—just an apple, some cheese, and a canteen of water. His stomach rumbled as he waited for some kind of signal. He had learned Morse Code as a boy and had his own shortwave radio at The Laurels. Fortunately, he was quite proficient.

At 10 p.m., he finally heard the first signal. He replied by putting in the days code. Fortunately, it was satisfactory, for the sender immediately began sending his transmission.

"Operation Sea Lion delayed. All-out bomber assault August thirteen—Eagle Day—to prepare for Operation Sea Lion postponed until following week when air superiority shall be attained by bomber action. Standby for further instructions."

The sender signed off. Christian relaxed and rejoiced. The RAF was proving a real barrier to the Germans. However, the bomber action sounded ominous. He put in a telephone call to Braden immediately.

D

The fifth of August came and went. Weather was bad over the Channel, so Goering's planned all-out assault was obviously delayed. Hannah sat at her station every day awaiting the "pre-invasion" wave of bombers. Then they received intelligence about something the Germans were calling "Eagle Day"—August 13. Invasion was to follow this sustained bomber attack.

When August 12th dawned clear, she was nervous. Weather had been bad. Would they strike a day early? She said a special prayer for Rudi. As she sat at the radar, the sudden surge of aircraft coming from France chilled her blood. Literally hundreds of bombers were headed across the Channel.

A great battle ensued, and she knew Rudi was somewhere in the mix. But the RAF was not able to hold off all the bombers. The radar demanded all her attention.

Then there was a huge explosion that rocked their command post, even fifty feet down. She put on her helmet and kept at her reporting. The screen was thick with planes.

All at once her screen went dark. Radar had been hit.

Every day they waited, Rudi's impatience grew. He even forced himself to find distraction in reading American murder mysteries—Raymond Chandler and Dashiell Hammett.

Then the day of the twelfth dawned clear. When the signal to scramble came, he was greatly relieved and anxious to test himself against the wave of aircraft coming from France.

As he rose into the air and went to the coordinates dictated by his headphones, the sight that met him caused the air to whoosh out of his lungs. It was an armada of *hundreds* of bombers and MEs. He started shooting, but only hit one bomber. The odd thing was that the MEs weren't breaking formation, even to engage the Spitfires and Hurricanes. They remained like a blanket over the bombers, which necessitated reducing the speed at which the fighters usually flew. Rudi calculated that they would run out of fuel at this rate. The bombers were larger and had a much greater fuel capacity.

As he returned to refuel, the air was black with planes. The airstrip where he was to land was being blown up as he reached it. Climbing back into the sky, he used the last of his ammunition to shoot the predator out of the sky. He then landed in the bumpy field adjacent to the landing strip.

All was in accelerated action on the ground. The fuel station went up in a fiery ball, rocking the ground beneath him. Planes that had landed before him were aflame. He steered his Spitfire and with the last of his fuel hid in a stand of trees to keep it safe from Jerry. Feeling helpless, he watched from afar and listened the next hour as his airfield, its hangars, and the planes on the ground were blown to pieces by Stuka bombers.

Then it was over. Rudi jumped out of his plane and ran to what was left of his station as the all clear sounded.

The claxon of arriving ambulances and fire trucks now rent the air, a relief after the whine of the Stukas. Rudi joined the survivors, hosing down the fires and dragging the wounded to the wave of ambulances that arrived to whisk them away.

Aircraft arrived, landing in the field with the very last of their fuel as he had done. The captain waved his arms in the direction of the forest, where Rudi's Spitfire was. However, most of the planes lacked the fuel to make it that far, and sat in the field—open targets should the Stukas return that day.

Fortunately, they didn't come. Not that day.

𝒟

Anthony received a summons to appear in the MI5 office of Roger Braden. It was not convenient, but Lord Halifax had counseled the entire Foreign Office to make themselves available.

The room in which their meeting took place was grim, without embellishments of any kind, and rather dark. He wondered for the first time if this were not an interrogation. Today Braden's square, gray-haired presence felt menacing.

"Mr. Fotheringill, would you be kind enough to give me the history of your association with Mr. Reston?"

Anthony cleared his throat. "That is a rather tall order. We have been acquainted since the war, where he fought bravely, I might add."

"Let us be clear." Braden rose from his chair behind the table where he sat. "Nigel Reston is a traitor. There is absolutely no doubt. We are no longer interested in determining his guilt, but in bringing in co-conspirators."

"Understood," said Anthony and endeavored to begin again. "My mind is still having trouble grasping the fact that I never really knew him."

"Who were his other friends?"

"The other men in the F.O., as far as I know. Our relationship was actually quite superficial, looking back. You see, I was separated from my wife for many years. He was not married. We went about together socially—to the Opera and the theater. An occasional meal."

"What did you discuss on these evenings together?"

Anthony tried to recall, but either anxiety had plundered his memory or there really was nothing specific to recall. "You know, it's odd, but I can't really remember. He certainly never mentioned Germany or a son. I knew about his sister, but he didn't talk about her. He visited her at least once a year on his annual holiday. She was the only family he had, as I understood it. Obviously, I was wrong."

"He never expressed admiration for Adolf Hitler to you?"

"Never." He paused, recollecting a recent conversation. "That is, I recall only one recent conversation where he said he thought, contrary to Churchill's suppositions, that Hitler had the entire Invasion strategy worked out to the last detail."

The questioning continued for another hour. Disconcerted by the fact that he couldn't recall ever discussing anything of substance with the man, Anthony further doubted his judgement in thinking of Nigel Reston as a close friend.

"Who are *your* close friends, Mr. Fotheringill?" Braden asked at length.

"How is this relevant?" Anthony asked, shaken by the question.

"Let me determine that."

"My closest friend is probably Dr. Andrzej Zaleski, a patriotic Polish émigré whom I also fought with during the war. But, wait a moment." Anthony leaned forward in his chair. "You mentioned Christian von Schoenenburg as one of your operatives. Zaleski is his stepfather.

"Other than that, my social circle consists of the chaps in the F.O., and a few childhood friends I see from time to time. I grew up in London, went to Harrow and Oxford, but don't have as many friends from that time as you would think. I lost a lot of them in the war."

Braden handed him a pad of paper. "If you could write down the addresses of the school colleagues, I would appreciate it."

Annoyed but realizing the necessity of this from Braden's point of view, Anthony complied and was then free to go. Was he mistaken, or did Braden fancy him as a co-conspirator?

Rudi was surprised at how quickly his airfield recovered from the raid. The damage wasn't as bad as it had looked. The exploding fuel tanks had made it look worse than it was. Huge lorries carrying petrol tanks arrived during the night. Graders evened out the landing strip. But the most amazing part was that when they awoke the next morning, there were six new Spitfires sitting there to take the place of the ones bombed on the runway the day before.

A smaller fuel truck made its way out to the forest to refuel the planes of those who had hidden there. Rudi repositioned his plane near the runway so it was ready to go when the next scramble was called.

Rain began to fall mid-morning, but to their surprise, they received the order to attack, meaning Jerry had come out despite the weather. When Rudi ascended through the clouds, he heard the heavy hum of bombers. When he finally got one in his sights, he was surprised to see no MEs escorting it. There were no MEs about anywhere.

The fighting was heavy, but they managed to shoot down most of the bombers before they made it to the coast. The bad weather persisted, giving the men more time to recover from the damage that had been wrecked on them the day before. No one discussed it, but everyone knew that when the fighting resumed, the heavy bombers would be sent in again. And again. This was no longer a matter of dogfights in the air. England was being attacked all along the coast. How long could the RAF hold off the *Luftwaffe?*

$\mathcal{D}$

Hannah was extremely anxious. Radar had been repaired for the time being, and she was able to see the huge number of planes not only over the Channel but now over most of southeast England. There would be occasional days off due to bad weather, but losses on both sides were heavy on the days that they fought. They experienced temporary blackouts in radar reception. She couldn't help but wonder how long the airfields could sustain the damage they were receiving.

Fortunately, on the days he didn't have to fly, Rudi wrote.

Dearest Hannah,

I hope you are not fretting too much. The fighting is heavy and we are sustaining quite a lot of damage as I am sure you know. However, I am well. Just exhausted. I have taken to sleeping underneath my plane. We fly so many sorties in one day, I have to catch my sleep when I can.

The chaps are absolutely splendid. Their spirits are always up. We feel most vulnerable when we are on the ground. Oddly enough, we feel almost invincible when we are in the air. I would rather be in the sky than anywhere else.

Anywhere else but in your arms, that is. It hasn't been that many days ago that we were dancing at the Savoy. But it seems as though it happened in another lifetime. I still wear your handkerchief inside my uniform, next to my skin.

Yours always,

Rudi

His letters brought tears, but at least, for now, he was safe.

As the more severely wounded of the pilots were sent to Guy's Hospital, Nika began seeing a great number of them in the early part of August. She and Amalia always checked the newcomers as soon as they could, looking for Rudi.

Most of the men were suffering from burns, some extremely severe. Many had been rescued from the Channel, but she soon became aware that the battle had shifted onto the airfields. The pilots were less optimistic but more pugnacious than they had been during the first days of the fighting.

She gritted her teeth with horror at the things she saw, but tried to be cheery for the sake of her patients. A few of them spoke French. The burns were a different type of wound from what she had seen in Warsaw, as though they were fighting a different war. By the end of each day, she was exhausted by her efforts.

At first, Nika was glad that Anthony didn't call or telephone, for she was too tired to deal with her feelings. However, as time passed, she began to wonder at his absence from her life.

Amalia suspected mischief on Sonia's part. "Depend on it. She is determined to keep you apart. I'll wager she has made up some tale about you and spun it for Anthony. I am going to invite him to dinner."

"Oh, Amalia, I am much too tired. Aren't you?"

"We have peaches from our trees, and I've ordered a pie. We also have potatoes and carrots from our Victory Garden, as well as green beans. We are going to have Victory Garden Stew with a bit of bacon. We must celebrate Rudi's victories. And Christians, as well. I have had a letter, and he couldn't give me details, but he's brought down a ring of conspirators."

Amalia was so enthusiastic, Nika found herself perking up. She took a long bath after tea which relaxed her back which was always sore from working at the hospital. Dressing in her electric blue suit, she began looking forward to seeing Anthony. She sprayed herself with some of her precious Shalimar from Paris.

When he arrived, Nika was immediately attuned to his anxiety. He ordered whiskey without his customary soda, and drank it straight down. To her dismay, he seemed to have difficulty meeting her eyes.

She noticed Andrzej and Amalia exchanging a worried glance.

"How is life at the F.O.?" Andrzej asked in hearty tones.

"Devilishly awkward, but I'm afraid I can't give details. Just to say, we're all under a strain right now."

"I think it would be odd if you were not," said Nika. "We are under attack. I don't mean to be an alarmist, but I can only wonder why they are holding back from bombing London."

"Our fighters are holding them at the moment," Amalia said. "But one wonders how long they can keep it up. They must be exhausted, and word has leaked out that the airfields and depots are taking quite a beating."

"Goering is still trying to prove air superiority so that they can invade," Andrzej said. "So far, it seems the RAF still has the upper hand. When he begins bombing London, I believe it will mean that Hitler has given up on the invasion idea."

"Why do you think that?" asked Nika.

"That will signal a change of tactics," said Anthony. "He will be trying to beat us into giving in—forcing a surrender. He will no longer be using the French model, expecting a whole, virtually untouched country to fall into his hands."

The idea of a *Blitzkrieg*, coming on top of her exhaustion, caused Nika to lapse into silence at the dinner table. She caught Anthony stealing worried glances at her, but after dinner, he excused himself and left without seeking a private word. Her hurt at this behavior merely added to her misery. He *was* avoiding her, and she had no idea why.

As they gathered to listen to the news in the drawing room, Amalia said, "Anthony was certainly on edge tonight. Do you suppose he knows something dire that we aren't being told?"

"It's possible, I suppose. But the War Cabinet runs a pretty tight ship. I doubt that Halifax communicates anything that doesn't have to do directly with the Foreign Office," Andrzej said, filling his pipe. "But I must say, I've never seen Fotheringill so shaken, even by Madge."

The news was not heartening. Fighter command was said to be holding out against increasing attacks on the airfields of South and Southeast England. The bravery and stamina of the pilots and air crews was extoled. Nika took this to mean that they were surviving the battle, but just barely. Rudi was a hardy soul, but she couldn't help wondering how he was coping with the exhaustion of the endless fighting and simultaneous bombing of his airfield.

Amalia had received a short note from him, which she had shared. Nika recalled that he had said "for the first time, I realized today that I've been killing men, not just shooting planes out of the sky. It was sobering. But I have avenged Father's death many times over."

That night, sleep was slow in coming to Nika, exhausted though she was. She tossed and turned, wondering what was amiss in Anthony's life and why he had chosen to ignore her.

Perhaps it has nothing to do with me. Maybe it is just the war. Maybe he does know something terrible that he dares not share with us.

At just that point in her cogitations, she heard the eerie sound of the air raid siren. Bombers were headed for London! Throwing back her bedclothes, Nika struggled into her dressing gown, terror numbing her hands.

Amalia knocked at the door. "The Anderson shelter, Nika!"

Throwing open her bedroom door, she met Amalia and Andrzej in the hall. They clattered down the back stairs, meeting the servants on the way. As they ran across the garden to the shelter, they heard an eerie whistle followed by an explosion.

Nika screamed. "It's the Stukas! God save us!"

Amalia put an arm around her and hustled her into the shelter. "That's east of here, I think. They must be bombing the docks."

Beginning to shake, Nika sank to the dirt floor of the shelter, curling herself into a ball and covering the back of her neck with her hands. Tears streamed down her cheeks.

It had come. *Blitzkrieg* had started.

{ 19 }

Anthony, Sonia, and their servants waited out the air raid in the cellar of their house. The bombing and the need to calm his daughter shook him out of his personal preoccupations: the sight of Nika's eyes—like a wounded animal's—as he left The Laurels that evening; the atmosphere of suspicion Braden had sown in the Foreign Office; the increasing certainty that he was being followed.

"Papa, can you tell where those bombs are falling?"

"It sounds to me like they are hitting the docks. Far away from here, darling." He held her close to him.

How was Nika bearing up? This was what she had feared. His desire to protect her was so strong, it was all he could do not to run out into the streets and over to The Laurels. He probably would have followed that instinct had his daughter not needed him so badly.

Sonia was trying to keep a stiff upper lip, but he could feel the tension in her body.

"Buck up, darling. It will be over soon. They will get low on fuel and will have to return to France."

He was right. Soon, the all clear siren was heard. Sonia eventually relaxed in his arms and he escorted her upstairs to her room.

Anthony was too tightly wound for sleep. Instead, he sat up smoking his pipe and drinking a large whiskey. Tonight was just the beginning. It was telling that all his thoughts had flown from his mind except for the desire to shelter and comfort Nika.

Let the confounded MI5 investigate him all they wanted! They wouldn't come up with anything. He had been foolish to let it get to him the way it had.

And much as he wished it could be otherwise, he would have to leave the comforting of Nika through the air raids to Zaleski and Amalia. Sonia needed him. She was obviously terrified. He couldn't leave her alone.

$\mathcal{D}$

Rudi's squadron and airfield were severely hit by Goering's new tactics. He felt safest in the air, where at least he could defend himself. He was making up to seven sorties a day. Once they were on the ground, they were subject to the never-ending day and night bombing. But he knew they must hold on. Time was running out for the Germans. Soon the weather over the Channel would prohibit the Invasion.

His sense of mission carried him through the difficult days and nights until, unexpectedly, his squadron was rotated to the north, a much quieter area. There, they were to train new pilots.

He resisted the change, even resented it. But when he settled in at his new, quiet airfield, he began to sleep again—long hours of exhausted, uninterrupted sleep.

He wrote to Hannah:

My darling,

They have temporarily moved us out of the action, so you can relax your worries about me for a bit. Unfortunately, now that I have time to think, I miss you terribly. I know that you are giving 100% to your job and probably losing sleep in all the bombing. I pray that you are safe.

I have heard that there have been a few raids on London, mostly on the East End. It is difficult not hearing from you and from my family. I can only pray for your safety. It helped when I was doing my bit in the air every day. But now I feel useless, although I must admit that I am getting more sleep.

I have begun worrying about you and Samuel in all my spare time. Surely you cannot think to marry him, Hannah. He is wrong for you in every way, except that he is Jewish. I think of our last evening together and dare to hope that you love me. If such is the case, you cannot marry another.

Being close to death clarifies things. I have not ever been much of a philosopher, but I have realized lately that the only thing that is worth fighting for is love. I take you up with me in my Spitfire, and you are what I think of when the battle is over.

Remembering you in our yacht at Dunkirk reminds me that you are every bit as brave as the chaps in my squadron. Thinking of you in your lab, using all that frightful intelligence of yours to bring penicillin to the market where it can help people triumph over infection reminds me that you are as compassionate a person as I have ever known. Thinking of you in my arms tells me that I can never feel for another woman what I feel for you.

I love you, Hannah Gluck.

Rudi

$\mathcal{D}$

As Christian set up camp in Reston's flat, waiting for incoming messages, he grew bored. He subjected the place to a thorough going over, eventually locating letters and pictures from his son Werner from the years when he was growing up in Germany.

The letters were full of praises for Hitler and the new hope and self-respect he was giving the Germans. Werner was very active in the Hitler youth in Heidelberg, where he lived with Reston's sister, Elise, and her family. He played the trombone in a military band, marching in numerous parades.

Christian felt the inevitability of war in those letters. He wondered what had become of Werner, if he was still alive. Reston was still being interrogated with hopes that he would reveal the names of his British colleagues, but his time was running out. His execution was set for September 2. He would be shot in the bowels of Whitehall in order to avoid the publicity of a hanging. Chris received no more communications, indicating that someone somewhere had gotten word to the Nazi contact that Reston had been captured. He remained in the flat, however, in hopes that someone might come for the radio.

One day in late August, he was boiling an egg when he heard a key in the door of the flat. Turning off the flame on the stove, he flattened himself against the wall behind the kitchenette's door. Looking about for a weapon, he seized the saucepan of boiling water.

The intruder was making his way quietly about the flat. When Christian judged that he was in the bedroom, he followed him, treading lightly. From the rear, he could see a man of medium height, dressed in a dark suit and hat. He appeared to be packing up the radio.

Christian stepped on a loose floorboard. It groaned and the man spun around, a pistol appearing in his hand. Throwing the boiling water in the intruder's face, Chris was not quick enough to avoid the man's shot. It struck him in the abdomen at the same moment that the intruder felt the boiling water in his face. The man screamed, dropping the pistol as he clawed at his face.

Christian doubled over as pain shot through his abdomen like a knife thrust. Clapping his left hand over the wound, he managed to grasp the pistol from the ground with his right and shoot the intruder twice in the chest. Both of them fell to the floor.

All he could think of was getting to the telephone. Braden was not scheduled to check in with him for several more hours. By then he might be dead. His stubborn spirit urged him across the cold floor.

My life is not going to be ended at eighteen by a traitor!

Fortunately, there was a bedroom extension. Despite the screaming pain, he made it to the bedside table. Pulling the instrument off the stand onto the floor, he rang Braden.

"Send an ambulance," was all he managed to say before he fainted.

Andrzej made an appearance on the ward just before Amalia's tea break. His brows were drawn, and his mouth set. He had grave news.

Blood drained from her face. "Rudi?" she gasped.

Her husband gripped her arm. "Be strong, darling. It's not Rudi, it's Christian. I've just had him in the operating room. I removed a bullet from his abdomen. No one knew he was my stepson, so I was allowed to operate."

She slipped into German, "Holy Mother."

"He has lost a lot of blood, but I am hopeful that he will make it. He is in recovery now. When he regains consciousness, he will be brought to your ward so you can nurse him."

Somehow, Andrzej maneuvered her to a chair where she sat abruptly. Her whole body was cold. "But what happened?"

"I intend to find out. He arrived here in an ambulance with another man, who is waiting downstairs. I don't know how much they'll tell me, but I'll try to get what details I can."

Nika came over to them. "What has happened? Is it Rudi?" She stooped down so that she could look into Amalia's face and hold her hand.

"No," she said. "It is Christian. He's been shot. Andzrej operated on him."

The woman's eyes went to Andrzej, who repeated what he had told Amalia. "Perhaps you can take my wife down to the canteen for some tea. Christian will probably be a while longer in recovery."

"Of course," Nika said. "Can you stand, dearest?"

Nika and Andrzej pulled Amalia to her feet. Her legs felt like noodles, but the idea of a bracing cup of tea spurred her to the lift, where Andrzej escorted them to the canteen. He left her with a kiss on the cheek. "I'll leave you with Nika for the moment, while I report to Christian's colleague and hopefully get some information from him."

𝒟

Nika fetched two cups of tea and laced Amalia's heavily with honey, which was more plentiful than sugar.

"Here you are, Amalia, dear." Her love for the gallant woman bubbled up inside her as she realized how much she had come to depend on her. Now it was up to her to be strong for her friend. "I know what a marvelous surgeon Andrzej is. In Warsaw, he was known as a miracle worker. I am sure that if anyone could help Christian, it is he."

"But abdominal wounds are so tricky. And they can easily become septic."

"That is where your nursing skill comes in. And you yourself told me how the sulfa healed Andrzej's infection."

Amalia's still, white face alarmed Nika. She rubbed her friend's cold hands between her own, trying to get some circulation into them. Somehow, she had to get her past this shock so she could care for Christian. She knew no one could give him better nursing.

"Amalia, I know this is a terrible shock. Let me get you another cup of tea." She walked up to the counter and ordered more tea and honey. Nika prayed silently for the wisdom to know what to do.

When she returned to Amalia, she said, "You need to pull yourself together. For Christian's sake. I know it is difficult. Actually, I cannot even imagine how difficult, but I know this is what you would tell me to do."

"But, Christian . . . I never knew he was even in danger."

"Perhaps it is just as well. You've had all the worry you could handle with Rudi, and you have done marvelously. I can't tell you how much I admire the way you carry on. You have helped me so much. You are a great model to me of endurance and strength."

Amalia's eyes finally focused on Nika. The woman was clearly lost in her pain. "Where is Andrzej?"

"He should be back any moment. He is talking with Christian's colleague, remember?"

"Oh yes. That's right. Here he comes now, thank God." Amalia's husband strode into the canteen and came over to where she sat, still rigid, but with more color in her face.

"Did you use the sulfa?" was the first thing she said.

"I did, darling. Don't worry. I did everything I possibly could. It's up to Christian now to regenerate. I didn't want to risk a transfusion, but he's receiving a saline IV to rehydrate him. And he has a morphine drip for the pain."

"Nika says you were talking to Chris's colleague. What did he say?"

"Just that Christian was gathering intelligence and was surprised by a traitor. Chris got him, but not before the spy got his shot off."

Amalia shivered.

"The work he has been doing is vital, I was told," Andrzej continued. "We can be very pleased with him."

"He takes after his mother," Nika said.

"It's true," said Andrzej. "Now, darling, I must get back to the O.R. I know you will want to stay with Christian tonight, but how about if I spell you at midnight? You've had a shock and you need to sleep."

"I'll stay with Amalia until you come, Andrzej. She needs looking after, as well," Nika said.

Christian was conscious when he came up to the ward. "*Mutti,*" he said. "You are not to worry about me. I am going to recover very well. I have your constitution."

She smiled at him gently and ruffled his hair. "I know you are, darling. I understand you are a hero."

"I was unprepared for what happened today. I should have been on my guard."

"Well, what counts is that you came about all right."

Nika could not believe the change in her friend. One would never know the shock she had had.

She was massaging Amalia's tense shoulders as her friend sat with Christian, watching for signs of fever, when the air raid siren sounded through the hospital. Nika's heart speeded up and her mouth went dry as she panicked.

"What shall we do?"

Amalia responded firmly, laying her hands over Nika's, which were now clenching her shoulders. "Christian can't be moved." Her voice sounded flat, final. "You might offer to help the other nurses who will be trying to get the more mobile patients down to the basement."

Terror raced through Nika's entire body. She almost blurted out that they were on the south side of the Thames, where most of the bombs had previously struck, but the sight of her friend calmly smoothing the blankets of Christian's bed, though she was powerless to protect him, galvanized Nika. She said, "We must make a shelter for Christian. Tables. We can use tables."

There were three tables on the ward. Nika ran to the first and pushed all of its contents on the floor, the clang and clatter nothing compared to the sounds the bombs could make. Using every bit of her adrenaline-induced strength, she dragged the heavy furniture across the room to Christian's bedside. The other nurses and aides in the room helped patients into wheelchairs and up on crutches. Amalia was covering her son with extra blankets.

When she reached Chris's bed, Nika said, "Help me put this thing up on its edge."

"What are you doing?" asked Amalia. "Have you lost your mind?"

"Making him a little hut to shelter him." She scurried off to get the second table. This one, she pushed and scraped along the wooden floor. Nika was sure she was leaving long scratches, but that hardly mattered at the moment. With Amalia's help, she put the second table on its edge on the opposite side of the bed.

"There's another, larger table in the dispensary," she said. "It will make a good roof. Can you help me with it?"

Amalia followed her into the dispensary. Nika made as though to shove the boxes and medicine to the floor, but her friend said, "These are important medicines. The patients may need them later. We must simply move them as quickly as we can."

Once this was done, they carried the table to Chris's bedside.

"Now we take the ends and lift it up over him, balancing it on the other two tables."

With effort, this was done, and Christian, who still slept under the influence of the morphine, lay in a partially enclosed shelter. At that moment, they heard the whistle of the first Stuka. There was an explosion not far away.

"We must take cover," Nika said, feeling calmer now that she had taken action. "Crawl under one of the beds!"

Amalia seemed to be sleepwalking. Nika thought she must have had one too many shocks that day. Her helplessness was familiar to Nika, but fortunately she had moved beyond that state herself. She took her friend by the elbow and motioned for her to crawl under the metal-framed bed next to Christian's. Getting under another bed herself, she covered her ears and waited for the next bomb.

They had not long to wait. It seemed as though there were a firestorm of bombs raining down on London tonight. This was not one or two bombers like in the past. This was a whole fleet. It was, in fact, *Blitzkrieg*.

Nika thought it would never end. After what seemed like forever, a huge explosion knocked out the windows and glass flew into the room. Then the wall began to buckle and fall. Great pieces of masonry landed on top of where she lay, followed by the partial collapse of the ceiling. She stifled her screams. They were safe under the sturdy beds. She prayed the tables over Chris had protected him.

By Nika's watch, it was an hour before the all clear signal sounded. When she crawled out of her shelter, everything was covered with billowing plaster dust and debris—chunks of masonry, shattered glass, ceiling tiles, and twisted, disconnected wires.

The only place that was clear was inside the enclosure they had built for Christian.

{ 20 }

Hannah received Rudi's letter the day after the huge bombing raid on London. She read it on her way to the bunker. When she came to the testament of his love for her, tears burned in her eyes and she had to sit down on a bench outside before taking up her post below.

Rudi thought he was not good with words, but he had proved himself wrong. The strength of his feelings penetrated her in a new way. She hadn't thought she could love him anymore than she did, but her heart stretched now to contain a greater love, and a wave of warmth and comfort washed over her. Regardless of what happened in the future, Rudi had become the great love of her life. She only wished she could tell him so. His news that he had been sent north, out of the worst of the fighting, was an enormous relief.

Folding up the letter, she put it inside her uniform and began the descent down to her duty post. She found the room in a barely contained state of frenzy. Apparently, the night had been a busy one. London had received heavy bombing.

Relieving the WAAF at the radar post, she asked about what had occurred.

"Hitler is apparently repaying us for our bombing raid on Berlin. The Stukas got through our fighter shield and were relentless last night. Fighter Command is going to have to decide how to deal with the problem."

As the day progressed, it became evident that the full force of the *Luftwaffe* had been unleashed. Bombing of the airfields continued and there was another daytime raid on London. Every single squadron, including Rudi's in the north, had been called upon, but they had arrived too late to prevent the bombers from getting through to London.

Her head throbbed with a growing migraine. Situated as she was, she heard Air Vice Marshall Park conversing with a subordinate she did not know.

"Dowding is becoming worried about the situation. Croyden and Biggin Hill are completely shut down. And we are losing too many pilots. Unlike Spitfires and Hurricanes, they can't be automatically replaced."

The subordinate said, "What can we do but fight?"

Worry pierced Hannah in a fiery shaft and the throbbing over her left eye grew fierce. What was to happen to Britain? Were they going to lose this war in the skies? Were they going to become so decimated that an invasion was possible?

Her hands grew clammy and she suddenly felt desperately ill. Dashing to the ladies' room, she made it just in time to lose her lunch.

It wasn't like her to lose her nerve, but when she returned to her station, she only had to leave again for the ladies.'

Her commanding officer asked, "Are you ill, Gluck?"

"Yes, sir."

"Go home and get some rest. There is a nasty flu going around."

"It's a terrible time for me to be sick, sir. I'm sorry."

"Go home and mend."

She was sick once more before she left, but this time there was nothing left to heave up. Dragging herself up the five flights of stairs, she had to rest on the bench outside the bunker before she continued the short distance to her quarters.

Tanner was already there, also ill.

"It's a beastly bug," she groaned. "Have you got a fever yet?"

Hannah felt her head. "I don't think so."

"It will come. Better get settled in bed. When Josephs comes home, she can get us some broth or something."

"Don't mention any type of food to me," said Hannah. She crawled up onto her bunk and burrowed under the covers. She was freezing cold even in her full uniform.

Her fever shot up by the time Josephs appeared. She had news. "Your pilot is here, Hannah. He's got a twenty-four hour pass."

She groaned. "Not funny."

"No! I'm dead serious. He's not allowed in here, of course, but he's waiting at the pub."

Rudi, here! Hannah flailed helplessly in her bed. "Of all the luck. I'm sicker than a dog. Would you take him a message?"

"You don't think you can get out of bed?"

Hannah said, "Feel my head."

Her friend did as asked and whistled. "You're burning up. How long since you've had anything to drink?"

"I can't keep anything down. Neither can Sandra. You had best stay away, Nellie. Tell my pilot that Churchill himself couldn't command me to get up."

"Anything else?"

"He might as well go to London to see his mother, so he doesn't waste his leave hanging around here. Can you bring me my pad of paper over there? I'll just jot a few words."

She wrote: "I'm sorry. There is so much I want to tell you but it needs to be in person. Please go see your mother and give her my best. And please, please be safe. Hannah."

The very last thing Rudi expected was to spend his leave in London. Speeding in that direction by train, he heard bombs falling all around them and prayed that they would not hit the train, which was surely their target.

He had been living for the sight of Hannah, and his disappointment at having to leave Uxbridge with only a note was keen. Taking the note out of his breast pocket, he read it once again. Then, wrapping it in her handkerchief, he replaced it in his shirt pocket. He was becoming vastly sentimental!

The Kentish countryside was changing from its pastoral loveliness. There were far too many places where German planes had simply jettisoned their bombs, finding themselves short on fuel to reach London, or being beset upon by Spitfires and Hurricanes and needing to lighten their load so that they could escape. Reminders of war were everywhere. It made him feel so helpless to be below while the bombers raged above, escorted by MEs and squadrons of Spitfires shooting them down. He saw some spectacular crashes during his journey but breathed more easily once the train pulled into King's Cross Station.

Rudi planned to surprise his mother at Guy's. During the taxi ride, he was shocked by all the bomb damage. The East End and the south side of the Thames looked particularly gruesome. Skeletons of brick and stone were all that remained of many buildings. Clean up crews were sorting heaps of rubble in the street. And this after only a few days!

When he arrived at the hospital, he was truly alarmed. The east side of the building no longer stood. Paying his driver, he raced inside. Men with the Home Guard stood before the stairway to prevent people from going up into the damaged building.

"My mother is a nurse here. My stepfather is a surgeon. I'm just home for a day's leave and intend on seeing them. Where have the patients been moved? That is where my mother will be."

His RAF uniform registered with one of the guards. "I guess you're plenty used to bomb damage. Go around to the north entrance and up the stairway to the west wing. Our chaps are helping to set up a new ward on the first floor. Mind how you go."

Rudi followed directions and soon saw his mother and Nika scurrying around, directing operations in the new ward.

"*Mutti!*" he said, walking up behind her. He realized he had almost been holding his breath in his anxiety. But she was all right, doing her duty in her calm, competent way.

"Rudi?" She spun around. "What are you doing here?" Her face had gone white.

"I've got leave for the rest of the day. Have to be back at midnight."

She embraced him, kissing him on both cheeks. "I am so glad to see you! You look very fit! And you've come in the midst of chaos, I'm afraid."

"Tell me what to do, so I can help."

"First you must see your brother. Follow me."

"Christian? What is he doing here?"

"He's a patient. He was shot yesterday morning. I don't know details."

This news sent him reeling. "Is he going to make it?"

"Things look better this morning. Andrzej operated on him yesterday and got the bullet out. The sulfa seems to have worked to keep infection at bay. But I'll tell you, Nika saved his life last night."

He barely heard her, as they had reached Chris's bedside. Surprisingly, with all the action around him, he was sleeping.

"It's the morphine," she explained. "Abdominal wounds are very painful. He's on a full dose for the first twenty-four hours, then we'll start to bring it down. But his blood pressure is re-covering, which is the main thing right now."

His brother was only a pale version of himself and, sleeping, he looked very young. "What have you been up to, old boy?" Rudi asked in a low voice.

Nika came over to him, bringing a chair. "Rudi! Hello! You look good," she said in her halting English.

He gave the woman a smile. "Thank you."

His mother said, "She is our heroine. Last night when the air raid sounded, I absolutely froze! I don't know what was wrong with me. Nika made a shelter for Chris out of tables, and as it happens, she probably saved his life. The windows blew out, the wall collapsed, and the ceiling came down."

He wished he could speak French. "Tell her that I saw the damage and she has all my gratitude for her quick thinking." Turning to his mother, he hugged her. "I am so glad you are all right."

"Nika forced me to take cover under one of the beds."

"Well, put me to work. You two must be exhausted."

"We're running on adrenaline, I think. Before I give you anything to do, you must go see Andrzej if he is between surgeries. Just go down the hall and follow the arrows to surgery. Ask for him at the desk."

Andrzej was very glad to see him. "Rudi! Good show! Have you seen Chris?"

Rudi nodded, and they clapped one another on the back. Zaleski led the way into his office. "You've been routing Jerry. Your father must be very proud."

Instead of going behind his desk, Andrzej sat next to him in one of two wing backed chairs. "It's good to see you," Rudi said. "That must have been a bad raid last night."

"If it had been a direct hit, the hospital would have burned. Amalia and Nika were very lucky, but I don't mind telling you, I was horribly worried. I was at home, sleeping when the raid began, preparing to take my shift sitting with Christian at midnight."

"It sounds like Nika really kept her head," Rudi said. "I wouldn't have expected that after what she experienced in Poland."

"We never know how we're going to react under fire. I learned that in the last war. Nika is a champion. Now tell me, what's it like flying a Spitfire? How many kills do you have?"

"It's unlike anything you can imagine. I don't have words to describe it. I'm sure I've been living off adrenaline as well. Shot down about ten, I think. It's hard to tell up there. Talk about chaos! Everything happens very quickly and then you're out of ammunition and you have to land and refuel. We've been on the scramble lately. On my last day before being transferred to a quieter zone, I had seven sorties."

"Flyers being worn down?"

"I think that's the worry, but the ones I know would rather be in the air fighting than anywhere else. I've enjoyed the rest, but I miss being in the action. We should be rotated back to the Southeast in a couple of weeks."

"Hannah?" he asked.

Rudi couldn't help a broad grin. "I have to confess that the reason I'm here instead of Uxbridge is that she's laid low with a stomach bug and a fever. But she's fighting a battle, too. We really depend on Uxbridge for intel on the approaching MEs and bombers. They're making all the difference in this fight."

"She's an amazing woman. Reminds me a lot of your mother."

Rudi grinned again. "Yes, sir." He shifted in his chair. "How is London faring in the bombing?"

"I fear it has only just started. But the British are amazing. Do you know, everyone goes to work, just as though it is a regular day? At night the theaters are open. And the restaurants."

"That doesn't surprise me." Rudi shook his head. "I've never known anyone with the courage of the pilots I fly with. It is an honor to serve with them."

Andrzej stood. "I need to check on Christian. Let's go see how he's doing."

Anthony's fears for Nika's emotional well-being had grown to such proportions that he couldn't help paying a visit to her in the late afternoon. He had been torturing himself with Sonia's words that the woman was much different than he thought. Anthony couldn't get another word out of her, and his imagination was not leaving him alone.

How is she different?

He intended to judge for himself, if he could. The man tailing him followed him to Laurel House. How long was that to continue?

They had experienced an episode of day bombing close to three in the afternoon. He had read in the morning paper that Guy's was badly hit. Anthony worried that it might have sent Nika over the edge.

She was taking tea with Amalia, Andrzej, and Rudi when he called. To his surprise, she not only looked fit, she looked positively blooming. To keep from staring at her, he switched his attention to the young baron.

"Rudi! How wonderful to see you! How long is your leave?" Anthony asked.

"I take the night train back after dinner," the pilot said. "It's good to see you, sir."

Anthony sat across from Nika, who was seated on the sofa next to Amalia. "Everyone is looking amazingly fit," he said. "Not many bombs on the West End, as yet."

Amalia embarked on a tale of a close call that Christian had suffered, followed by his surgery and the efforts of Nika to save him during the bombing at Guy's the night before.

The recital left Anthony stunned. He could not belief Nika had displayed such *sang froid* when she should have been terrified by her memories. She had obviously proven herself in battle and jumped an enormous hurdle.

"I am impressed, Nika. Well done! That was thinking on your feet."

"It is surprising what a person will do when faced with danger," she said. "The whole plan was there in my head in a split second."

"While I was petrified with fear," said Amalia. "I am so glad Nika was with me. I probably would have done something useless like throwing myself over Christian's body."

"None of us have had much sleep," said Andrzej. "But Christian is on a lower dose of morphine now and the danger of infection grows less as the hours tick by, so I think he can be moved tonight if there is a repeat of last night's bombing."

"How about if I sit with him tonight so that you can get some sleep?" Anthony offered. "If Jerry lets you, that is."

"That would be more than kind," Amalia answered. "We've moved the ward to the first floor from the third. You will be able to get down to the basement with him if there is an air raid."

"Were there any casualties last night?" he asked.

"Two," Andrzej answered. "Patients who were too ill to be moved, and not enough people to put them on stretchers. Thus we feel especially grateful for Nika's acts in saving Chris."

Amalia switched to English for Rudi's benefit. "The hospital charity is rounding up volunteers to sit with any patients who might need a stretcher. It is amazing how people are coming together and rallying round."

Anthony felt tremendously heartened by her words and was glad that this little band of émigrés had come to appreciate the British character.

"It was difficult, but I have convinced Sonia to go into the country for the duration," he said. "She is staying with her mother, so I shall be quite free to sit with Chris tonight. Don't worry about a thing."

"In that case, you must stay to dinner," said Amalia. "You haven't had a chance to visit with Rudi."

{ 21 }

Nika was confused by Anthony's presence. Until he came, she had been basking in the evidence that she had moved beyond her terror of the bombing, and she had actually felt happy. But after he arrived, after having not seen him for so many days, she felt awkward and aware of the fact that she had not had sleep, changed her clothes, or washed since yesterday morning. He kept looking at her, and she hadn't a clue what he was thinking. Their easy camaraderie and certainly their romance seemed a distant memory. With all the crises they experienced and met each day, the events of war would seem to have stretched out time. The months of July and August had seemed endless, and here it was September now. She no longer knew what she wanted or where she stood with regard to Anthony.

Finally excusing herself from tea, she went upstairs and ran a bath. It was heavenly to soak herself in the tub. Her mind went to the changes she had seen in Anthony. He was as attractive as ever, but the lines from his nose to the corners of his mouth had deepened. There were new purplish circles under his eyes. But then, she probably looked even worse. None of them had been sleeping well with the air raids.

It was different here in England. In Warsaw, the Germans had been on top of them. The border had been so close, and there had not been a channel between them. And they had been invaded. The bombing was incessant. It had never stopped. It remained to be seen what this country would be like if the Germans succeeded in breaking down the RAF and invading the Island.

She wouldn't think of that now. The British were stronger than she had supposed. It might never happen. What was that phrase from the Bible? "Sufficient to the day is the evil thereof."

After her bath, her exhaustion claimed her. She could scarcely summon the energy to put on clean underthings as well as her dressing gown. Stretching out on her bed, she meant only to take a short nap, but ended by sleeping blissfully until the next morning. Only when she woke did she find out that she had slept right through another bombing raid.

Rudi rejoined his squadron, feeling as though he had been away a long time. Seeing his brother had sobered him in a way he couldn't explain. Fighting the enemy each day as he did had made Rudi feel invulnerable. He had certainly never expected Christian to be shot and nearly killed in what he had thought was the safer occupation. It had impressed upon him that fact that one never really knew what awaited them each day. There were no guarantees.

He wrote Hannah the day after his return.

Darling,

I was most terribly sorry to find you ill! I hope you are quite recovered now. As much as I would have like to have seen you, it was a good job that I went home. Chris was badly wounded in some hush-hush affair he was involved it. He was only just coming around from the morphine when I left him. We got very sentimental, I'm afraid. I know it seems strange, but neither one of us thought to be in that situation. Mother and Andrzej say that he will recover completely, thanks to the sulfa. And, of all things, thanks to Nika, who has turned heroine. There was a bombing raid on the hospital the night following his surgery, and she erected some kind of shelter over his hospital bed that Mutti says saved his life. I am beginning to think that you never know people until you go through a war with them.

London is experiencing severe bombing, and I feel responsible for it. We cannot seem to down enough bombers before they break through to London air space. We have our hands full, trying to protect the air bases and London at the same time. I long to be back on the front lines.

I missed you in London. The family did not seem complete without you. I hope next time I have leave, we will be able to go there together.

All of my love,

Rudi

The next day, word came through that they were being rotated back down to the southeast, where the fighting was increasing. Jerry was throwing everything he had at them, some felt in a desperate show to bring the British to their knees before it was too late to invade. Hitler had been enraged by the bombing of Berlin.

As he flew his Spitfire back to Biggin Hill which, who knew how, had been brought back into full operation again, he flew by instruments through a heavy fog. It was coming to be autumn soon. Weather was definitely a factor Reichsmarshal Goering couldn't command.

Rudi thought of each member of his family. Being away from them had distilled certain pictures in his mind. His mother—deceptively fragile, but tempered steel. He never recalled her as anything but strong, even when Father was murdered, but she had almost lost her bearings when Chris was shot.

Christian—sunshine, devil-may-care, brilliant, but apparently not invulnerable. He wished he knew the story there. Come to think of it, *Mutti* had nearly come undone when Christian was the family's first victim of the Nazis back when he was ten. He had been clubbed during a raid on the neighborhood Jewish bakery. She had nearly caused civil war between the government and the Nazis over that incident.

Andrzej—wickedly handsome, he stood as a stalwart guardian of Rudi's mother, their relationship extending to back before time began. He could be expected to take care of *Mutti* if something should happen to her RAF pilot son.

And, lastly, Hannah. Red for passion and his heart's blood. Courageous, compassionate, intelligent—he loved her more than anyone who drew breath. What would become of her if Jerry caught him in his fire and caused Rudi to go down? Would she marry Samuel? He sincerely hoped not. That threat was a good enough reason to stay alive, should he find himself in a tight spot.

Biggin Hill appeared below him. He needed to cease these maudlin thoughts that were so unlike him and concentrate on things that were to hand. Jerry needed to go down. And soon.

As soon as they landed, the bell rang for a scramble. He had no time to think. He went back into the air. Rudi had never seen so many of the enemy. There were several hundred of them in the sky at once. Most of them were bombers, with MEs escorting them but not engaging the Spitfires in combat. Rudi shot through them to the bombers, aiming for their cockpits. He shot one down, but that was only one of hundreds. Before he ran out of ammunition, he positioned himself with skill and shot down another bomber.

He was on his way back to base to refuel and get more ammunition when a force of MEs flew over him. He had no ammunition left. He dodged and tried to get above them, but the *Messerschmitts* always had the advantage in that maneuver. Flying north, he hoped he could tempt them to come after him and run out of fuel.

Over a forest somewhere out of his normal zone, his plane took a direct hit. Shrapnel flew everywhere, injuring his face, slicing through his bomber jacket, cutting up his arms and chest. Blood was in his eyes, and the plane was on fire. Shouldering his parachute, he bailed out. Somewhere below, his Spitfire crashed and exploded. Rudi free-fell through the air, deployed his parachute, and was relieved when he felt it catch the wind. Floating down, he could hear the distant sounds of battle.

Hannah didn't know when so many planes had been in the air at once. There were hundreds of Jerrys, and every RAF squadron had flown into the battle to keep as many bombers as possible from reaching the airfields and their manufacturing targets in London. From what she was able to tell, there were heavy losses on both sides.

She became aware partway through the raid that Churchill himself was standing behind her, watching the lights go on above her head as each squadron took wing. All the lights were on now which meant that all the squadrons were in the air. The radar was a mass of signals, and still wave after wave of MEs, Stukas, and Heinkel bombers kept coming.

Where was Rudi? He was somewhere in that massive fight. Would he continue to live a charmed life? Or would he go down in the Channel to die of hypothermia before he could be rescued? Perhaps his body would be blown to bits inside his plane. Her eyes blurred. He was only one among hundreds, and a significant part of them were falling from the air.

She hadn't been the same since the day he had come to see her. Over and over again, she had wished she could have seen him, even if she had had to crawl. She needed to tell him that she loved him. If he were to die, she wanted him to die knowing that he had her heart.

If the Prime Minister himself were not standing behind her, she didn't know if she could have continued to sit there until the enemy, at last, went home.

"When will we know how we did?" Churchill asked in the voice everyone in England would recognize. Last time she had talked to him, she had been with Rudi. It had been before the PM was even in the government. He had commended their bravery in dealing with a renegade SS officer who had tried to shoot them after raiding and destroying her lab at Oxford.

"It was a costly battle, but we sent them home before they wanted to go, I think," Vice-Marshal Park said.

"Just out of curiosity," Churchill said, "how many did you have in reserve?"

"None. All our chaps were in the air."

Slowly, all the light bulbs on the board above Hannah's head went out. It was a solemn couple of moments, and Hannah wouldn't have brought herself to Churchill's attention even if she had wanted to.

"An epic battle," the Prime Minister said.

"Yes," Park replied. "We gave them everything we had."

That night, as Hannah lay in her bunk, she longed for sleep that would not come. Normally, she would be exhausted at the end of such a day, but not tonight. She was deeply disturbed. No one needed to tell her that they couldn't fight many more battles like the one today. Was there no end to the German planes? German pilots? German bombs?

How many epic battles could they fight?

Then she heard it. Planes taking off. Not Spitfires and Hurricanes. Bombers. The drone of their engines became more distant. They were off to night bomb the enemy.

Christian woke slowly from his drugged sleep. Had Rudi really been here? Or was it some kind of hallucination? Someone was here now. He turned his head.

"Von Schoenenburg?" It was Braden.

"Yes, sir."

"How's the wound?"

"Better, sir, I think. They're keeping me pretty drugged up. My mother is head nurse on this ward." He felt as though he were moving through heavy water.

"Good. Good. Thought you'd like to know we identified your assailant. He was a cipher clerk in our own branch."

"From MI5, sir?"

"Yes. He's gotten away with a good deal of information over the years. But he wasn't very smart about his fellow travelers. They were well known to be his friends. There was a corps of about six of them—all different branches of government, ready to step in and do their bit as soon as the Jerrys landed. Used to drink together at the Yellow Hound."

"Are they talking?"

"As fast as they can. They think for some reason that if they give one another away, things will go easier for them. But no matter how they try to dress things up, it's treason." Braden's mouth was flat and grim. Then it softened unexpectedly as he looked at Christian. "Sorry you've had this spot of bother. Good job your stepfather is a first-class surgeon."

"I'm going to be fine, sir."

"Get well, then. We need you. The proposed dates for the invasion have come and gone, but last anyone heard in our little group of spies, it was on for October."

Christian hated his uselessness. "Do you really think they can pull it off that late in the year, sir?"

"There's more than one philosophical difference between Churchill and Hitler, of course, but in this case the operative one is that Hitler would probably push ahead, no matter what the cost to his troops if there were any chance he could succeed. But one thing he knows: without air superiority, and with the

Royal Navy still in control of the Channel, he hasn't got a hope in hell."

When his chief left, his mother came to his bedside. Her face was drawn and pale and he cursed himself for having given her worry. "How are you feeling, darling?" she asked.

"I think I might do better without the morphine."

"Let me just check your blood pressure." She fastened the cuff over his arm, pumped it up, and then read the gauge as the cuff slowly loosened.

"It's still a bit low," she told him. "But you're healing nicely. I can change the morphine solution so that you are receiving less, but I'm not quite ready to take you off of it altogether."

Christian had never seen her in her nurse persona before. She was formidable. "When you are discharged from here, you are coming home to recuperate," she told him. "It is going to be painful for you to walk for a while and you will be weak from lying in bed. We are all very lucky that you got to the hospital when you did. You could have bled out lying in that flat."

He smiled at her. "Yes, it was very careless of me to get shot, wasn't it?"

Her eyes were stern. "I think there is a guardian angel assigned to you, but don't try him too hard."

"From what Andrzej has told me, one of my angels is Nika. Imagine her being so resourceful!"

"She saved my life as well. I was frozen to the spot when the air raid siren sounded, I was so frightened. All I could think of was that you couldn't be moved." His mother wiped her eyes. "Well, I'll just slow your morphine drip here. But be certain to tell me if you are in too much pain. The more pain you are in, the slower your healing will be."

"I just don't like feeling as though my life is happening at a distance."

"I understand, darling. Now, that's done. I will just begin my rounds."

ⅅ

Amalia and Nika went home alone that afternoon. The air raids in London and along the coast had resulted in a backlog of surgical cases that seemed to grow by the day. Andrzej was needed at the hospital. Amalia worried about his long hours. She had noticed gray hairs among the black ones in his thick hair.

She also missed his comforting presence during what had become the nightly air raids. Actually more concerned about his location rather than her own, she tried to hide her anxiety from Nika and the servants.

As she poured out tea in the afternoon ritual, she listened to Nika.

"Do you notice that Anthony has changed?" her friend asked.

"Changed how?" Amalia sipped her tea and then spread honey on her bread.

"He seems distracted, not his normal, calm self."

"There was an upset in his office of some kind, but Andrzej says he is not meant to speak of it. Maybe that's it."

"It could be. He can't seem to sit still for long."

"Well," said Amalia, "he waited hours for you to come down last night. I told him finally that you had fallen asleep. He acted disappointed."

"I haven't seen him for a while, but I was very tired."

"I think Sonia has sown discord between you. Perhaps it is best that she has gone to the country."

When they had drunk their tea, Amalia stood. "I think I will try to take a nap before the bombs start falling."

"How blasé you sound. Quite like an Englishwoman," Nika remarked.

"I'm not, really. Just trying to keep my head."

The bombing that night commenced during their dinner and lasted for a long time. As Nika and Amalia held hands in the Anderson shelter, they cringed at every explosion.

"There can't be much left of the docks," Amalia said. "I pray they stay away from the hospital."

"I hope the British are plastering Berlin and the industrial parts of Germany," Nika said, her voice hard.

A whistle close to them was followed by an explosion not far away. "That one was pure hatred. They have no reason to attack civilians."

"They're monsters," said Nika, wincing at another close hit.

The door opened and Andrzej came stumbling in.

Amalia's heart went to her throat. "Darling! What were you doing coming home in an air raid? Are you hurt?"

"Not a scratch," he said, crouching by Amalia and taking her in his arms. "I didn't want to leave you two on your own."

"But you could have been killed!"

"I ran quickly and came by the tube. There are crowds of people down there. I'd say it makes a pretty good shelter. They're playing cards, dancing to the fiddle, some are even sleeping."

She said no more, she was so glad to have his arms around her and to be resting her head on his chest. Remembering all the years she had been without him, she thought that if there were a single time she could have chosen to be with him, it would be now. Now with both of her sons in danger, with a city around her in flames. Previously, she had only experienced war from hospitals away from the front. She had never been under threat of losing her own life. She had never had sons fighting.

They got little sleep that night. Huddled together as they were, they slept in fits and starts between the bombing runs. In the morning, when Amalia went for a shower to wake herself up, she found that they had no water.

"Our water main has been hit," she informed Andrzej. "We'll have to wash at the hospital."

"Bother," he said. "Is that the door? Who can be calling at this hour of the morning?"

"It must be important,"Amalia said. "I'm dressed. I'll go down."

When she reached the ground floor, she found Sims just coming out of the butler's pantry, a telegram on his silver salver. Alarm suffused her, halting her in the entryway. The butler came to her, and taking the telegram from his tray, she slit it open with her fingernail.

DEAR MRS ZALESKI: AM SORRY TO INFORM YOU YOUR SON WAS SHOT DOWN YESTERDAY AND IS MISSING STOP ALL EFFORTS BEING MADE TO RE-COVER HIM STOP

CAPTAIN JOHN J. REYNOLDS

Amalia's ears rang louder then fainter then louder again as she stood trying to take in the telegram.

Is he dead? Is this just a softer way of telling me he's dead? Did he fall into the Channel? Did he go down and burn with his plane? Are they trying to find his body? Or do they think they might still find him alive? Or was he picked up by Germans and put in a camp?

Sinking to the floor, she crushed the message in her damp hands, vaguely aware that Sims had left her. The black edges of the room began to come together, until all was black and her head hit the carpet.

When she came to herself, she was in Andrzej's arms and he was carrying her up the stairway. For a moment, she forgot the message, then it hit her once more. Biting her bottom lip, she stared ahead, unable to process any thought.

Andrzej sat in the overstuffed chair in her boudoir, holding her across his lap with her head on his shoulder. Taking the pins out of her hair, he ran his fingers through it, stroking her.

"Darling, darling, darling. Most of the pilots shot down jump out in their parachutes and are recovered. Don't fret just yet. They have been very busy over on the coast. I doubt they have been able to spare many men to look for him. I am nearly positive that Rudi will turn up."

Amalia was completely numb and had begun to shiver. Her thoughts were chasing themselves, but she couldn't speak. Bunching Andrzej's shirt in her fists, she burrowed into his chest.

Nika entered the room. "What is it?" she asked.

"Rudi has gone missing," Andrzej said.

Walking swiftly across the room, she knelt by Amalia's chair. "Dearest, he will turn up. I'm certain of it. If there is anything your sons are, it's enterprising!"

"Perhaps you had better go down to Guy's," Andrzej said. "Give the attending surgeon the news, and the head nurse as well. We, neither of us, will be in today."

"If that's the most helpful thing I can do, I will. I think I will also order her strong tea with honey." She bustled out of the room.

I can't bear it if he's in a German POW camp! How will I even know? Or what if he's lying wounded somewhere and no one finds him? What if he dies of hypothermia in the Channel?

Her thoughts would not quiet, but she remained dry-eyed. Andrzej continued to stroke her hair and kiss her hairline, murmuring positive thoughts. "He will be found, darling. He will find a way to survive." After a few moments, he added, "He's a man in love, don't forget. I think we should wire Hannah. She needs to know, so she can add her prayers to ours. I will tell her to get compassionate leave and to come down here to us. You would like that, wouldn't you?"

She nodded.

{ 22 }

Hannah was just leaving for her shift when a telegram arrived for her. Who could be sending her a telegram?

Opening it, she stood stock still as she read the dreaded words.

RUDI SHOT DOWN AND MISSING STOP KNOW NO FURTHER DETAILS STOP PLEASE JOIN US IN LON-DON IF YOU CAN GET LEAVE STOP DR ANDRZEJ ZALESKI

Hannah crumpled the telegram in her hands, crushed it into a ball and threw it across the room. "No!" she shouted. "No! This can't happen!"

Nellie Josephs looked up from their tiny vanity mirror and ran across the hut to her friend, taking her in her arms. "Hannah, is it Rudi?"

"Yes! It can't be happening, Nellie! It simply can't! They say he's missing!"

"Who says?"

"His stepfather—Dr. Zaleski. They've invited me up to London. I must go. I must get leave. I need to be with them."

"Of course you do. You can get compassionate leave. Tell them he's your fiancé and you must go to be with his family. Go now to the C.O."

An hour later, Hannah was on the train to London, though her real desire was to be combing the Channel and the countryside for Rudi. If anyone could find him, she could, but she would never be allowed in the area.

Rudi, darling, I love you. You must know it. You must feel it. Come back to me.

She whispered the words in time with the clack of the wheels on the railroad tracks. Her hands were doubled into fists.

How could she have thought she would not marry him when given the chance? How could she have thought she could go forward in this world without him?

Memories swam through her mind—the first time he had kissed her on the outside steps to the clinic, the day they had gone punting in the bright sunshine down the Cherwell, the incongruous sight of him playing Bach on his violin. She longed with her whole soul to feel the comfort and excitement of having his arms around her. She wished she could see his confident smile and the way the sun glinted off the auburn of his hair.

He must have gone down during all that fury and madness yesterday. There were a lot of planes that went down. They must be having a lot of trouble accounting for everyone. If only I could help search. I would find him.

When she at last arrived in London, she took a bus to a stop near Mayfair and walked to The Laurels, carrying her small case. Sims greeted her at the door and showed her into the doctor's library.

He was there alone, sitting with his pipe in hand, staring blankly out the window.

"Ah, Hannah. There you are. This is a dreadful business, but I feel sure Rudi will turn up."

She went to him and offered him her hand. He shook it firmly. "Thank you for inviting me. I would have gone mad if I'd had to stay in Uxbridge alone with news like this."

"Amalia is upstairs. I gave her a sedative and she is sleeping. She's being very brave. But then, she always is."

"May I see the telegram?"

The doctor fished it out of his pocket and handed it over to her. Brief. To the point. Nothing more than what she already knew.

"I must make myself useful," she said. "I can't just sit around."

"Do you garden? We have a small Victory Garden and I was just about to go pull weeds and harvest some carrots and Brussels sprouts for dinner. I, too, need to be occupied, but I don't like to leave my wife."

Hannah had never worked a garden in her life. "Be glad to help," she said.

They walked outside into the garden, and the doctor handed her a pair of outdoor gloves. He carried a bucket and a basket.

"I don't need to tell you that Rudi is very resourceful," Hannah said. "And he doesn't give up or give in easily."

"You are right, Hannah. I am counting on him to turn up in one piece. He is also a good pilot. He already had a crash that he lived through the first day he was in battle."

They knelt in the plot that was a little more than small. It took up a good portion of what must have been the flower garden.

"Show me the weeds," she said. "I've never been around a vegetable garden."

The doctor indicated a row of uneven plants between the rows of vegetables. "Be sure you pull up the roots, too."

They worked in silence for a few minutes. The doctor was harvesting not only carrots and Brussels sprouts, but beets and little red potatoes.

"I love Rudi, but he doesn't know it," she said finally.

"Oh, he knows it," said the doctor.

"I'm going to marry him."

"I imagine he knows that, too."

"No. He thinks I'm going to marry Samuel. And there is no legal marriage between Jews and Christians in Austria. He must go back there. There's the barony."

"There may not even be a barony after the war, Hannah. Let's not borrow trouble."

𝔇

Rudi came to consciousness to discover he was hanging in a tree by his parachute harness. Shaking his head, he thanked God he was still alive.

Surveying his situation, he realized he was still about thirty feet from the ground. He was covered in blood and could barely see. Both eyes appeared to be swollen almost shut. His chest, arms, and abdomen were still bleeding, but his first priority was to figure some way of getting to the ground.

If he merely cut his harness off, he was going to fall straight down. Looking at the branches surrounding him, he realized that he was wedged between two stout oak branches. That was luck. He was weak, but he was going to have to manage to climb down the tree somehow.

Reaching for his pocket knife, he sawed the thick canvas of his harness with one hand and clung to one of the branches by looping his arm over it with the other while holding the harness steady. When one side of the harness fell away, he was able to loop his right arm over the other branch and shrug out of the left side of the paraphernalia. He was left hanging by his right arm. He threw his left arm over the same branch and tried to find purchase for his feet. Slowly he worked his way down. When there were no branches left, he dropped the last ten feet and rolled, spraining his ankle with a jolt of pain that shot through his leg like lightning. He lay gasping and weak on the ground.

Rudi examined his wounds. A head wound still bled into one of his eyes. There was a high wound in his abdomen that could be trouble. Altogether he hurt like billy-oh, as his comrades would say. It would be the easy thing to just give up and fall asleep here in the forest. But he couldn't do that to his mother or Hannah. Not while there was still life in him. He reached down inside for the determination he knew was there and told himself that he was not done yet. He was going to see that he did whatever it took to make certain he survived.

Getting up on his hands and knees, he began crawling through the thick trees towards the fading evening light. When he reached the outskirts of the forest, he found himself in a field planted in rows of wheat. He needed rest. He needed sleep. But no one would see him lying here, even if they were looking.

With his last bit of strength, he pulled off his jacket and laid it wide open on the field so the white sheepskin lining showed. Shivering there in the dirt, he lost the fight to remain conscious.

$\mathcal{D}$

"Where is Mother today?" Christian asked when his stepfather was making belated rounds.

"We've had some news," the doctor told him. "Rudi's plane was shot down and he's missing. She collapsed. You and I both know she's a strong woman, but she hasn't been sleeping with all the bombing. I insisted she stay home."

The news was a shock, but he rallied quickly. "Poor *Mutti.* But as for Rudi, I'm quite certain he's all right."

"You are, are you?"

"Less than half the pilots shot down are actually killed," he said, hoping he sounded confident.

Andrzej just sat there, as though lost in his own private melancholy.

"Well, thank the good Lord you are going to be all right, at least," he said finally. "I know I'm not your father, but you and Rudi are the closest thing to sons I will ever have. I'm proud of you; I pray for you. I don't think your mother could bear to lose either one of you. In addition to her love for you, you are her connection to your father."

"Rudi, especially. He looks like a larger version of Father."

"How are you doing with the morphine?"

This seemed an abrupt change of topic. "I was going to ask mother to discontinue the drip today."

"How would you feel about coming home and finishing your recuperation in your own bed? I think it would do your mother good to have you there."

"That would be smashing. I'm ready to get out of here. And I'd like to be with *Mutti* now."

"Hannah has got leave and she's there, as well."

"I like her, Andrzej. How is she taking it?"

"She is very positive, but it's a strain for her. It will be good to have you there."

Andrzej took Chris home in a wheel chair and taxi at tea time, and they arrived just as the daylight bombing began. Chris was in more pain than he wanted to admit. The doctor escorted him to the shelter where Amalia and Hannah were ensconced with the servants.

"Christian! Darling!" his mother embraced him carefully and kissed him on both cheeks. "How good to see you. But, Andrzej, what about the morphine?"

"He claims he doesn't need it any more. We don't want to make him dependent, and to be frank, the beds are needed."

As he listened to the eerie whistle of the Stukas and the following explosions, Christian thought about what he had heard about the battle during which Rudi was shot down. The more severe burn cases had reached the ward that morning, and the pilots had been talking. They said it was the worst day of the battle, that Jerry had hit them with everything all at once. Hundreds upon hundreds of planes.

"Hannah," he said. "It's good to see you, though the circumstances are rotten. How long is your leave?"

"Only seventy-two hours, and I was lucky to get that. Things are especially chaotic at the moment. I can only hope we have some good news before I have to report back. Maybe someone saw him go down."

"The odds are good that he survived. I've been talking to the chaps in the hospital. They say that only about a third of the pilots that get shot down are killed," said Chris.

"Rudi has excellent survival instincts," Hannah said.

"Like *Mutti*. She escaped from the Gestapo in Salzburg."

Just then a bomb exploded close by. The ground shook and the little lantern hanging from the ceiling took to swinging. His mother gripped his hand. "That was close! Where is Nika?" she asked Andrzej.

"She decided to stay for another shift. They are shorthanded. She knew that Hannah, Chris, and I would be with you."

His mother said, "I think we are only now beginning to see the real Nika. The battle has brought the best out in her, surprisingly."

"I never would have expected it," said Andrzej. "People can be quite surprising."

"It's because she's Polish, like you. Never say die," said Chris.

Then he heard his mother tell Hannah the story of the night after his surgery when Nika saved his life with three tables. "Before that, she was absolutely traumatized by the bombing, and now, here she is working right through it," his mother concluded.

"Hitler has met his match in the English people. It is good for all of us to be among them right now," said Hannah. "Someone will help Rudi. I know they will."

{ 23 }

Rudi came to consciousness as rain fell on his face. Surprised to find he was still alive, he took heart. He heard voices—a man and a woman.

"The pilot who rang said he may be strung up there tangled in his parachute."

"If he came down in those trees, we might never find him," the man was saying querulously.

"Oi," Rudi managed to call. "Oi!" His pain had leached him of hope. Would they even hear him?

"I hear something, John. Over there it was. Look! I see something white."

Soon a woman wearing a raincoat and boots discovered him. Relief suffused him as he looked into her homely face.

"Oh my stars. He's badly shot up." Her cool hand rested on his head. "He's got a fever and he's all over blood. Get the wagon, John. We'll have to take him home in the wagon."

Her husband harrumphed and marched off. As the wife fussed over him, Rudi passed out once more.

When he came to consciousness the next time, he was tucked up in clean white linen in a bed in what looked to be a low-beamed farmhouse. The farmer and his wife were looking at him with hard suspicion in their eyes. His wounds were still undressed and he was burning with fever. The man stepped back and pointed a game rifle straight at his chest.

Surely this is some type of hallucination. I am obviously in a bad way.

"Don't you try anything," he said. "The police are on their way."

Rudi closed his eyes once more. "*Wasser,*" he moaned. "*Bitte, bringen Sie mir Wasser.*"

But no one brought him water. The next time he awoke, the pain was searing his left eye and the wound in his abdomen. Why had no one called a doctor? He was still burning with fever. He could only see through a haze. What appeared to be a beefy looking policeman sat by his bed.

This must be real. But what has happened? What sort of thing could cause the police to come? Why wouldn't they at least give him some water?

"A chap from the Home Office is on his way," the policeman said, heavily. "Though it appears you might not last that long. Ugly looking wound you got in your belly. And unless I miss my guess, you've got an infection in them eyes of yours. May go blind."

Home Office? What was he talking about? I'm going blind? Why aren't they doing anything to help me? I'm dying of thirst. I probably am dying, actually.

"Captain Reynolds," he managed. "RAF."

"You can't fool us. You're no captain. You're a Jerry is what you are. Your uniform won't fool us. You come to spy on us."

Rudi realized then that he must have babbled in German. Hopelessness overtook him in a debilitating wave. He hadn't the strength or the clarity of mind to explain.

The blackout curtains were up. He had no idea how much time had passed. He was so dreadfully thirsty . . .

"Get this man a doctor!" someone thundered. "How can I interrogate him when he may be mortally wounded and he's burning with fever? Have you even given him any water?"

"He's a stinkin' Jerry!"

"Water! Doctor! Immediately!"

Rudi opened his eyes. His head felt as though it were splitting open. He couldn't speak. Soon the farmer's wife was raising his head and pouring water between his parched lips. He drank eagerly. She poured him another glass. He drank again. Maybe he wouldn't die.

Hannah. Mutti. I can't die.

He had no way to judge the passage of time. His vision was so impaired, he couldn't even make out the features of the Home Office man. Everything was a blur. But he heard a soft noise and realized the man was going through his clothing. Then he was looking at the identification tags around his neck.

"Von Schoenenburg. Funny that he would use a German name. I swear the name is familiar, too. Hmmm. Von Schoenenburg."

The doctor finally arrived. He was a terse man. Probably not thrilled to be working on a Jerry. He spent what seemed like hours digging shrapnel out of Rudi's abdomen, face, chest, and arms.

"Sulfa?" Rudi managed to utter.

"You want sulfa do you? Well I have some, but it seems a waste of good medicine to use it on you when you're only going to be shot."

"Please?"

"Do it," the Home Office man said.

With bad grace, the doctor sprinkled sulfa in his wounds before stitching them up.

"He may lose his sight. Shrapnel imbedded itself near his eyes and the infection spread."

"Just do your best," the Home Office man said. "Mrs. Biddle, bring him some more water."

After he had taken two more glasses of water and the doctor had left, he felt the tags being removed from around his neck.

"Leave him to sleep," the Home Office man instructed Mrs. Biddle. "I'm going into the village to use the telephone. I have some calls to make."

When next he woke it was night again and bombers were droning overhead. He was still feverish, but he no longer felt quite as hopeless. He knew the miracle of sulfa because he had seen it heal his stepfather from a nasty infection and save his life. He prayed it would do the same for him.

He lay thinking of Hannah and his mother. No doubt they had been informed he was missing. They must be going through tortures. Hopefully, he would be more coherent when he talked to the man from the Home Office.

As though he had willed him to appear, the man walked into the room and turned on the light.

"Your C.O. is involved in a heavy battle, so I haven't been able to question him, but I did call the Home Office about you. Your brother is Christian von Schoenenburg, isn't he?"

Rudi nodded.

"I learned about your family. You are close personal friends with the PM, for one thing. Austrian émigrés. Lost your father to the Nazis in 1938."

Rudi nodded with relief.

"I apologize deeply for what you have suffered. Mr. Biddle heard you babbling in German and jumped to the obvious conclusion. Now our first priority is to get you better care. We must try to save your vision. I want you to travel to London. To Guy's."

"Stepfather is a surgeon there," Rudi managed. "Mother a nurse."

"Then that is just the place for you. I am going back to London and will travel with you. If it weren't absolutely necessary, I wouldn't move you. This is going to be uncomfortable. Farmer Biddle will take you to the station in his wagon. I've reserved us a first class compartment, so you can lie down across the seat. Going from here, it isn't a hospital train. We'll get you an ambulance once we reach London."

Rudi nodded. "Thank you."

"We'll leave on the first train in the morning. Get some sleep."

$\mathcal{D}$

Amalia was teaching Hannah how to knit.

"I find it helps me to have something to do with my hands," Rudi's mother said. "It's really a mindless sort of thing, once you learn how."

Hannah was trying her best to learn, but she had never been good with handiwork of any sort. And her mind was so consumed with Rudi that she couldn't really concentrate.

Is he lying wounded somewhere, dying alone in a field?

"I appreciate your trying to distract me," she said. "But wouldn't you rather be at the hospital? What if they bring Rudi in?"

"I would rather be here with you, darling," said Amalia. "We share this dreadful bond. We don't even need to talk about it. We know what each other is feeling. I cannot believe that you still intend to marry Mr. Weissman, you know."

"No. I shan't. Even if . . . even if Rudi were not to come home, I wouldn't marry him. It was all mistaken loyalty to my Papa. It is Rudi I love. It always has been."

"It is clear to anyone that you are in love. Don't make the mistake I did, Hannah. Marry the man you love."

The words shocked her. She had always supposed that Rudi's mother had loved his father deeply.

As though reading her thoughts, Amalia said, "I grew to love Rudi's father. But our marriage started as one of convenience. There was a terrible misunderstanding between Andrzej and me, but he was the man I had loved since I was a girl. Both of us were too prideful. Times were different then. Society had strict rules. It was very important that one played by the rules."

"It doesn't bother you that I am Jewish?" Hannah asked.

"It is a complication, yes. But I think very highly of you, Hannah. You bring out the best in Rudi. You are intelligent and compassionate. You have every quality I could wish for in a wife for him." A spasm of pain crossed her face. "Let us pray that you have the opportunity."

Hannah sought for words to divert them from negative thoughts. "Rudi says that your closest friend in Vienna was Jewish."

"Yes. Rosa Gruen. We nursed together in the first war. We became very close. She was the only one who knew what my feelings for Andrzej had been. During all the years I was married to Rudolf, we never spoke of it, but just knowing she understood was a great comfort. She and Andrzej had been very good friends at the hospital, as well. She knew my dilemma, knew the things I could never admit even to myself."

"What became of Rosa?" Had she fallen victim to the raging anti-Semitism in Vienna? Hannah almost hated to ask.

"She escaped to Switzerland months before I did. She was going to Luzerne. If we had been there longer, I would have tried to find her, but, as it happened, we were only there a few days, as you know."

"I am glad she is safe," said Hannah. "Too many Jews clung to their homes. They made themselves blind to what was happening around them. They didn't really comprehend Hitler's hate."

"It is so irrational that it is hard for intelligent people to comprehend," Amalia said.

"Now, I think we must try to eat some luncheon." She looked at Hannah's attempt to knit. "You weren't just being modest!" Amalia actually laughed. "There is really something you can't do, isn't there?"

Hannah grimaced. Then she heard the heavy knocker on the front door.

Amalia perked up immediately. "Perhaps it's another telegram! Perhaps they've found Rudi."

Unable to wait for Sims, they both set aside their knitting and tried not to run down the stairs to the front hall. A man stood there with Sims.

"A Mr. Williams, Madam," Sims said, handing Amalia a card on his salver. "From the Home Office."

"The Home Office?" Hannah and Amalia echoed in unison.

"Yes," Mr. Williams said. "I have important news about your son, Rudolf."

Hannah couldn't stop herself, "What kind of news?"

Amalia intervened. "I am Mrs. Zaleski, Rudi's mother. This is Hannah Gluck. Will you come into the sitting room?"

They entered the coral-colored room which seemed bright and hopeful to Hannah, even with the rain outside.

"I won't keep you in suspense," he said. "Your son is alive, though not in the best of shape right now."

Amalia threw her arms around Hannah in a spontaneous embrace. Hannah hugged her back. Rudi's mother began to shake with sobs.

"Let us sit down, Mr. Williams. Where is Rudi?" Hannah asked.

"I left him at Guy's. His most serious wounds are one near his eye and in his upper abdomen. Dr. Zaleski is treating him."

Amalia gulped one final sob. "I must go to him!"

"What are his chances of survival?" Hannah asked bluntly. She was stepping out onto hopeful ground only tentatively.

"I am not a doctor. He has had a harrowing time. He was rescued by a farmer and his wife, who mistook him for a German spy. That is how I came to be called in. Fortunately, we got things sorted out once I got there, but they hadn't called a doctor or even given him water. He was infected and running a high fever. He had lost a lot of blood. The train ride to London was difficult for him, but I knew enough to know Airman von Schoenenburg needed the best medical care."

Amalia's hand went to her mouth, and Hannah's stomach clenched with dread.

"Thank you, sir, for coming and informing us yourself," Hannah said, as Amalia seemed incapable of speech. "What did Dr. Zaleski say about his condition?"

"I won't try to bundle it up in clean linen. It is critical."

Hannah's mind was racing. "I might be in a position to help. I worked for the lab where a new drug called penicillin is being readied for the market. It is a miracle drug in the fight against infection. I'll ring them."

{ 24 }

After informing a recuperating Christian of the hopeful news, Amalia and Hannah took the Underground to Guy's. It was the middle of an air raid, but they knew that the Underground, once reached, was the safest place for them. It was filling up with people seeking safety. It never occurred to Amalia to stay home in the shelter.

Funny how I don't even flinch at the air raids anymore.

The All Clear sounded as they emerged from the station and hurried down the street to Guy's. They went directly to Andrzej's office, but he was in surgery. Amalia led Hannah up to her ward on the first floor. She had changed into her uniform, determined to nurse her son herself.

It was surprisingly difficult to find Rudi. Nika had come home that morning to rest after working all night, so even she was not there to guide them. They went to bed after bed, and finally found him, his entire head swathed in white gauze bandages. His arms and torso were also wrapped. Alarmed, Amalia exchanged a glance with Hannah, who was clenching her jaw.

Amalia took Rudi's hand in hers and motioned Hannah around to the other side of the bed to take his other hand.

"Rudi?" she whispered, "It's *Mutti* and Hannah."

When he did not respond, she checked his IV bag.

"Morphine. And it's set at a pretty high dose. He's sleeping. He must have been in a lot of pain."

"I must speak to Dr. Zaleski," said Hannah. "Dr. Florey said penicillin is ready for the market, but they only have limited quantities. If the doctor wants to use it, I can go up to Oxford to get it."

"Yes. Let's speak to Andrzej." Amalia squeezed Rudi's hand. "At least Rudi's here. I think we owe Mr. Williams a huge debt of gratitude. Think of him in that farmhouse with no treatment! Not even a drink of water." Tears burned in her eyes at the thought of what her son had endured. "But I'm so glad they found him," she said. "He was probably delirious and babbling in German."

She watched as Hannah brought Rudi's hand to her lips and then held it next to her cheek. Listening to her speak softly to Rudi in their native tongue, tears streaming down her cheeks, Amalia decided to leave them alone. She needed to find Andrzej as soon as possible.

"His condition is critical, darling," he said. His right eye is seriously infected. I stitched his wounds, but I fear he will have a scar on his face."

Amalia bit her lip. "His vision?"

"It's too soon to say. His left eye is still good."

"What about his abdomen?"

"I had to repair his duodenum, but the most danger to him now is from infection. I'm afraid of septicemia. That shrapnel was in there for hours before the doctor finally got it out. He's also lost a lot of blood. He was severely dehydrated. "

"Hannah needs to speak to you. She wants you to try penicillin. She can go up to Oxford to get it. Remember the clinic where she worked? She knows the doctor in charge and he's willing to give her a supply."

"I'll speak with her immediately. I won't mince words with you, darling. That could save his life."

Amalia gripped her hands together, striving to feel her professional calm, but this was Rudi they were talking about.

"I can't lose him, Andrzej. I just can't."

He pulled her into an embrace, and she felt herself melt into him. He kissed her temple. "Don't give up on him, darling. He's young and he's strong. And with penicillin . . . well, from all I've read, it's a miracle drug. Thank God for Hannah."

Hannah was so grateful she had been given leave. As she traveled to Oxford on the train, she knew very well that Rudi's life probably depended upon this errand of hers.

The countryside north of London was pock-marked with bomb craters, particularly near the airfields. It saddened her, for one thing she had loved about England was the idyllic nature of its countryside. Because it was a wet climate, it was always green with flowers blossoming everywhere, charming streams and wooded dells. Now it looked like another planet.

Her preoccupation with Rudi had given her temporary respite from her concerns about how long London and the rest of the country were going to be able to endure Hitler's fury. But now she thought of it. How many other pilots lay in similar condition to Rudi?

His condition was particularly bad because he had been so far from the main action and hadn't gotten help for far too long. But penicillin could help anyone with wounds. The early trials of the drug which she had read about in medical journals in Switzerland were the whole reason she had chosen to go into biochemistry. But never had she known it would make such a personal difference in her life.

Dr. Florey was a handsome man—square-jawed, with rimless glasses. He read the letter she carried from Dr. Zaleski describing Rudi's condition.

"Our supply of oral penicillin is not large, but we can make more," he said. "I would not feel good about withholding it from this brave young man when it has a chance of saving his life. How are you involved, Miss Gluck?"

"He's my young man, sir. If he lives, we are going to be married. He is also from Vienna. We met in Switzerland after his father was killed by the SS. His brother was also recently shot by a Nazi sympathizer, but he seems to be recovering."

"It sound as though the family has been through a lot. It is an honor to help. I am only glad that we can."

He gave her several boxes of capsules. "Give him two in the morning and two at night for as long as they last. Keep me informed of his progress."

"Thank you so very much Dr. Florey." Though she was in the seat of clinical professionalism, Hannah found she could not stop tears of gratitude.

Defiance

The train ride to Oxford and to Rudi had never seemed so long. Hannah prayed as she rode, hoping that he could hold on—that his youth and former good health would carry him through the day.

I couldn't bear to lose him now. Please God, help him to survive. Help him hold on until I arrive. Help him to tolerate the penicillin. Help it to work its miracle.

There were no bombs falling when she arrived, so Hannah splurged on a taxi to carry her straight to Guy's. When she arrived, she went straight up to the ward.

Nika and Amalia were holding a conversation with Rudi. His mouth and nose were the only parts of his dear face that weren't bandaged.

"Hannah is here," Amalia announced. "She has brought the penicillin."

Standing at the foot of his bed, Hannah was suddenly overwhelmed by the extent of his injuries. Tears welled again in her eyes. "Rudi," she said, her voice hoarse. "Dr. Florey has kindly given you enough penicillin that it should cure your infection. They didn't have much. That is their problem—they haven't been able to manufacture it in large quantities. But there should be enough here. Can you drink, darling?"

"Come here," he whispered. "Let me feel your face."

Replacing Nika at his side, she took his right hand, kissed the palm, and held it to her cheek. He traced her nose and mouth with his fingers. "It's been so long," he said.

Hannah scarcely noticed as the other women moved off. "I love you, dearest Rudi. And you are going to get better and we are going to get married. As soon as you are able to stand."

"Andrzej says I may lose the sight in my right eye."

{ 223 }

"That doesn't matter to me. The only thing that matters to me is that you live. Now, I'm going to pour some water, and you are going to take these capsules. Two right now, and then two later tonight."

The head of his bed was cranked up, so she put the glass of water in his hands and then put the capsules on his tongue and guided the water to his mouth. He gulped everything down.

"Not every man has a woman with magic powers." He smiled. "I wish so much that I could see you."

"Soon, darling, soon."

"And what about poor Samuel? Does he know we are to be married?"

"I broke things off with him weeks ago, it seems. I don't remember exactly when. Time really has no meaning right now. It is just getting through one day at a time, isn't it? They all blend together."

"You have made me very happy, Hannah. In spite of everything. I have loved you for so long. I feel as though I am floating."

"That's the morphine, darling."

They laughed, and it felt better to Hannah than anything had for a very long time.

{ 25 }

Rudi heard the volunteer stretcher bearers, to be employed in case the air raid sirens went, drinking coffee and playing cards on the first floor landing as he penned his letter.

Dearest Hannah,

Since I am writing this letter, you will have gathered that the bandages are off and I can see. Both eyes have healed, and I thank the Lord above. I have been taking the penicillin for a week now and all symptoms of septicemia have gone. My many wounds are well on the way to being healed. Only today did I learn how grave my situation was.

I thought I was prepared for blindness, but when I saw my mother's anxious face as the bandage was removed, I knew I wasn't really. However, I hope you are fond of "dueling scars," as I shall have a nice approximation on my right cheek.

I am aware of the great debt of gratitude I owe you for your connection to Dr. Florey. My thanks will never be enough. It is another miracle that you were here. Dr. F has been in touch with my stepfather about my progress, and trains permitting, will make a trip up to London to see me. As you probably know, the railroads are being bombed pretty thoroughly and are always in a state of repair. Thank God you were able to get up to Oxford and back in a timely manner.

How are you carrying on? I understand that the bombing is being focused on London now, giving the air bases a break. The bombing here is fierce. When London is rebuilt, it will be a different city. Guy's is becoming structurally less sound, and they are looking for another place to remove the huge number of patients. Our ward already has thrice its normal number. Whenever the bombs are not falling and the fire sirens aren't wailing, you can hear the sound of construction. The feeling of "pressing on" and prevailing never dies among the English.

I think Hitler's bombing raids now are motivated by pure pique. He knows he will not be able to invade this year, or maybe ever. The great Luftwaffe was flummoxed by our little lot. No one knows better than you how we have been outnumbered. My mother has made a sign bearing Churchill's iconic statement that hangs next to my bed: "Never in the field of human conflict was so much owed by so many to so few." It has been a great honor to be one of the few, and I look forward to resuming flying when I am back in shape. There are two times when I feel wholly alive: in the air and whenever I am with you. It is a great regret that I cannot combine the two and take you up in the air with me. (Though

I would not like to expose you to the MEs no matter how much you might wish for it!)

Now, to us: Remember that you made the statement that you were ready to marry me as soon as I could stand? I always knew that when you were ready, you would propose to me! So! I am to begin walking around the ward tomorrow and to go home shortly after that. When can you get leave? Shall you mind getting married amidst bombing raids? Perhaps, if you have leave, we can take a short honeymoon to Scotland.

All my love always,

Rudi

Nika worked as many hours as she could manage. The numbers of wounded increased daily, and she understood that these were only the worst cases. Doctors were going out in the streets, patching up those who had lesser injuries. Amalia and Andrzej worked long hours, as well. The days of taking tea together at home were long past.

She didn't think about when it would be over. No one seemed to. They just carried on as best they could. Parliament sat every day, moving from chamber to chamber. Downing Street was bombed, but Churchill simply moved underground to the annexe.

She did wonder more and more about Anthony. The longer she went without seeing him, the more awkward she imagined things to be.

One morning, just as she was entering the hospital, he caught up to her.

"Nika! I was hoping to see you."

Thrown off her purpose as well as her stride, she merely responded, "Anthony! What are you doing here?"

"I wanted to see you. I heard from Andrzej last night that you saved Christian's life in an air raid. That you have apparently become fearless! I have been wondering how you have been enduring this never ending rain of bombing."

She smiled and allowed him to take her arm. "Let's catch a quick cup of coffee in the hospital cafeteria." As they walked down the stairs to the basement, she said, "Really, I have only been carrying on, the same as everyone else. You were right. The British are unique. I don't think they will be beaten."

"It doesn't mean the Poles are in any way inferior," Anthony said. "It's all a matter of geography. We allow ourselves to believe that no one can cross that channel."

After they had their coffee and sat down in a corner table in the cheerless room, he said, "I have news."

Startled, she looked up at him. He was smiling, but his eyes remained serious and fixed on hers.

"Whatever is it?" She asked.

"I'm being posted to Egypt with an important task force."

"Egypt?" The word startled her. "Why now?"

"The Suez Canal is of vital importance to this country, especially during war. We cannot allow the Egyptian government to close it for any reason. No doubt there will be a fierce war in North Africa, but Hitler may work on the country diplomatically as well. My task force is being sent there to wine and dine the Egyptians and keep them friendly to us. No doubt there will be Germans there as well."

Nika's eyes went wide. She couldn't imagine Anthony going that far away in the middle of the war that was waging here in Britain.

"But traveling is so dangerous!"

"We will fly out of Scotland to neutral Sweden. Then we will fly South from there. Jerry isn't concerned with air traffic out of either place at the moment."

Her heart thudded with anxiety. "I will worry about you. Is there any way you can let me know that you are safe?"

"I will send you a letter through the diplomatic pouch. It will probably take a while to arrive, though, so don't take to worrying."

Impulsively, she grabbed for his hand across the table. "How long will you be gone."

"It depends upon the war. It could be awhile, Nika. I just don't know."

She tried to compose herself. *I am not going to cry!* "I will miss you dreadfully. How is your daughter?" she asked.

"I suspect Sonia of mischief-making. What did she tell you about me?"

Nika was startled by the direct question. "It doesn't matter. I knew it couldn't be true."

His face was grim. "What did she say, Nika?"

"I don't want to cause problems between you and your daughter," she said, feeling cornered.

"I need to know what she said. It's important. If she's telling lies, I need to know. And I don't want anyone to damage my relationship with you."

Nika sighed. "I didn't believe her. She is jealous, Anthony. The last thing she wants is for you to marry again. You must see that. But let's put it behind us. You are leaving for who knows how long."

After staring into her eyes for a few moments, he said, "You are right. And I leave tonight. I refuse to leave you without kissing you good-bye."

"This cafeteria has become the scene for many a drama. No one will think anything of it," she said, smiling tremulously.

Standing, Anthony raised her to her feet and took her in his arms. "I will miss you terribly."

"And I you. But I am braver now. You don't need to worry about me."

"I can see that." He brought his lips down on hers and kissed her soundly while she gripped the sleeves of his jacket. "But I want you to take all precautions to be safe."

"And you! When I think of Egypt, I think of far too many dark alleys."

"You do have an imagination, don't you?"

"And sultry Egyptian women."

He kissed her again and her knees grew weak. "No worries there. Good-bye, darling,"

"Be safe!" Nika said. "And please go before I start to cry."

Putting the back of her hand to her lips, she watched him walk across the room and prayed that would not be the last time she would see him.

Epilogue

It was as though dark clouds parted and the sun shone brightly the day Hannah was married. She stood next to Rudi in the Registrar's Office, Christian at his side and Amalia at hers.

Though thinner, Rudi still looked every inch the aristocrat—even more so with the "dueling scar" which she secretly thought quite appealing. She had a bouquet of yellow roses, ordered especially by Rudi to be sent in from a hothouse in the country.

There were not enough coupons for a wedding dress, so she wore her uniform, as did Rudi. She gazed at his beloved face throughout the short ceremony, more grateful than ever that he was alive and there at this moment.

When they were pronounced man and wife, they kissed for the first time in two years. Hannah felt warm and safe, as though she had come home from a long journey. With Rudi's arms around her and the prospect of a week's leave in Scotland, away from all the bombs, she felt as though she were in some kind of heaven.

One kiss was not enough, and at his second kiss, she felt passion stir inside her, passion only Rudi could raise. Putting her arms around his neck, still holding her bouquet, she pulled him closer and indulged herself. She had waited so long for this.

When they finally pulled away from one another, she felt as though her surroundings had dissolved. There in the Registrar's Office with the fragrance of furniture polish and roses, she had become Rudi's wife, and that was all that mattered in the whole, crazy world.

The End

Historical Notes

According Winston Churchill, from September 7th to November 3rd, an average of two hundred German bombers attacked London every night. Mysteriously, the bombs on London stopped for a season, never to return with that intensity. This period is known as "The Blitz." Through the winter of 1940–1941 the bombing of other key cities in Britain took place.

We know now that during all this winter, Hitler had turned his eyes from Britain and was planning his invasion of the Soviet Union. That was always his first interest, though he said otherwise to Stalin and the Soviets.

Because he didn't invade or conquer Britain, history declares that England won the Battle of Britain. It was the first time Hitler lost a battle. The fact that England withstood the great *Luftwaffe* is considered a miracle.

I had exceptional resources for the writing of this book. First and foremost was *Their Finest Hour*, by Winston S. Churchill. Other sources included: *The Miracle of Dunkirk*, by Walter Lord, *The Churchill Factor*, by Boris Johnson, *Never Give In!*, *The Best of Winston Churchill's Speeches*, selected by His Grandson, Winston S. Churchill, the excellent television documentary "Battle of Britain—One of WWII's Most Significant Battles," by Espresso TV, UK, and *The Eagle Unbowed: Poland and The Poles in The Second World War*, by Halik Kochanski. Another source, not to be ignored, was my "Blitz Experience" in the Imperial War Museum, London.

Other Books in this Series

The Last Waltz

It is December of 1913 in Vienna and Amalia Faulhaber is surrounded by the whirlwind that is the life of a nineteen-year-old socialite. She is comfortable and confident in her wealth, her heritage, and most of all, in her engagement to the Prussian baron, Eberhard von Waldburg. All this comes crashing to a halt the day that her fiance informs her that their engagement is off since he is returning to Prussia to fight in what he is sure will be a glorious war.

Thus begins the tale of a heroine of extraordinary background and resource who develops into a woman who would be extraordinary in any age.

The men in her life—a German officer in World War I, a patriotic Polish doctor, and an Austrian Baron, all shape her, but more remarkably she shapes them. Her utopian socialist uncle has raised her with ideas outside those of the upper classes, imparting to her a more complete picture of the day than possessed by the other men in her life. This quality causes her to champion the Austrian Democratic Experiment and to especially mourn its demise.

The Last Waltz is full of little known history of a land that was, in 1913, the apex of the worlds of science, medicine, art, and music. The speed with which the five-hundred year old empire fell, and the reasons behind that failure carry many warnings for the world we live in today.

Exile

It is 1938, and Austria has just fallen to the Nazis. Amalia von Schoenenburg's husband, Rudolf, has been murdered by the SS before her eyes. Fleeing to Switzerland with a vital message from Rudolf for Mr. Winston Churchill, she is accompanied by her two sons and Dr. Andrzej Zaleski, the man she loved heart and soul before the Great War. As this little band of exiles works to complete its vital mission, Amalia struggles with grief and guilt. She loved her husband and raised two children with him, but how can she deny the passion that has existed, hidden away--the passion of a lifetime?

About the Author

G.G. Vandagriff has been a scholar of 20th Century Central European History for many years. She received her bachelor's degree in International Relations with a concentration in Central Europe from Stanford University. Desiring more in-depth study, she completed a rigorous Master's Degree program at George Washington University in the same subject.

In 2009, Vandagriff published the award-winning *The Last Waltz: A Novel of Love and War*, drawing on her studies while living in Austria and studying the politics and history of that country with Austrian professors. In that novel she introduced the characters of Amalia, Andrzej, and Rudolf, taking them through the Great War and beyond to the *Anschluss* of Austria by Germany. *Exile* marks the beginning of a series of books that will take these characters (and some new additions) through the Second World War.

The author of twenty books, Vandagriff writes in many different genres. You can become acquainted with her mysteries, romances, and women's fiction at her website http://ggvandagriff.com.

She has lived all over the country, but she and her husband David now live on the bench of the Wasatch mountain range in Utah. They are the parents of three children and grandparents of five delightful grandchildren.